D1527742

THE OTTO DIGMORE
DECISION

BRENT HARTINGER

BOOKS

BK Books
www.brenthartinger.com

Cover design by Philip Malaczewski

ISBN-13: 9781699611951

For Michael Jensen

Still the best decision I ever made.

CHAPTER ONE

Desperation smells like sour sweat, unwashed socks, and garlic.

Garlic? Who eats garlic before an audition? Well, I did once, but only because I ended up being told about the role at the very last minute.

My name is Otto Digmore, I'm twenty-nine years old, and I'm sitting in a waiting room on the Paramount lot before an audition. There are four other actors with me, and I'm wondering which of us is the source of which smell. Is any of it coming from me? I put on Gold Bond Ultimate Comfort body powder this morning, but you can never put on too much, and I'm hella hoping it's doing its job.

We're all auditioning for the same role in an upcoming remake of *It's a Wonderful Life*.

No, not the George Bailey/Jimmy Stewart part. Word is an offer's already gone out to Chris Pratt for that role. We're auditioning for Adult Harry, George Bailey's brother. George rescues him from drowning as a boy, and he later becomes a war hero, saving all those lives that otherwise would have been lost if George hadn't saved *him* as a kid. I haven't read the whole script—this new, updated version, I mean—but from the "sides," which are the pages of the script they give the auditioning actors, I can tell the story is basically the same.

I'm as tired of movie remakes as anyone, and the idea of remaking classic movies like *It's a Wonderful Life* seems especially boneheaded. Do they really think they are going to improve on something that's already so good? Problem is, audiences love remakes. Not always, but often enough that they do better than most original stories. And until that changes, Hollywood is going to keep grinding them out. It's like how people always say they hate it when politicians throw mud at each other, but then go ahead and vote for whoever throws the best mud.

Anyway, being in a big studio movie with Chris Pratt would be an amazing credit, and it can only help my acting career, even if the movie ends up being terrible and forgotten in five minutes. Especially if it makes money.

I could stand to make some money too. That's what all the actors in this waiting room are thinking: How great would it be to land a role in a studio movie and finally make some real money? None of us cares if the movie turns out to be a piece of crap. We're reading for the role of Adult Harry, who only has sixteen lines. But none of us is A-list, or even B or C-list, so we can't afford to be choosy.

The actor sitting directly across from me—a guy with a blond buzzcut—nods at me. I nod back, even though I suspect he's the source of the garlic smell. Is it his breath, or is it coming out of his pores in the form of sweat?

I've never seen him before. I do recognize the faces of the other three guys, because the same actors always get sent out for all the same roles. I don't know their names. I have my earbuds in, even though I'm not listening to anything, because I hate it when guys get chummy in the waiting room before an audition. Either the guy's a bundle of nervous energy, which I don't need in my head, or he's trying to gauge the competetion—maybe even trying to find a way to shake our confidence. It's a competitive business, and some people will do whatever it takes to get ahead.

Some of my acting friends complain about how distracted they get in waiting rooms, because casting directors often want a specific "type," so the actors end up surrounded by mirror images of themselves. Or, worse, they're surrounded by guys who look a lot like them but are just a little bit better looking.

That's never been an issue for me. All four guys here are way better looking than I am, just like always. And one of the guys is Asian, and another is black, which is interesting, because we're reading for the part of Chris Pratt's brother. In the last year, I've seen a lot more people of color at the auditions I go out for. I'm white, so I guess that means casting directors are more open to non-white actors now, even for roles that aren't written specifically for them.

Go, diverse casting!

I've wanted to be an actor ever since high school, when I played the Fool in a production of *King Lear* by William Shakespeare, and I turned out to be pretty good. I moved to Los Angeles right after college, and a couple of years ago I got cast as Dustin, a supporting character in this college sitcom called *Hammered*. We were cancelled after only a single season—it was kind of a bad show—but it gave me a little taste of what life is like as a successful Hollywood actor.

"I hear they're going for a really gritty take," Garlic Breath says to the Asian guy. I'm pretty sure the second guy is the one who smells like unwashed socks.

"People don't remember," Unwashed Socks says, "but the original was pretty dark. Jimmy Stewart hates the world so much he tries to kill himself."

They're violating an unspoken taboo by talking to each other before an audition, but I perk up at the word "gritty."

"Yeah, but I hear they wanna go even darker," Garlic Breath says. "Make it relevant for *now*. Show that the world really has gone to shit, but that's all the more reason to believe one person can make a difference."

At this, I can't help but get excited. I said before I don't worry about seeing my own doppelganger at auditions, but it's not because of the race thing, or the looks thing. It's because I'm a burn survivor. I have a big scar on the right side of my face, and more scars on my neck, and also on my shoulder and chest but that's usually covered by my clothes. It happened when I was a little kid. I was fooling around with some gasoline in the garage, and I set myself on fire. I guess you could say it's kind of defined my life, but that's hard to say since I don't know any different.

Racial diversity is one thing. Casting a guy with scars on half his face is something else. My scars have made it hard to get acting roles in Hollywood. It's not like there are a lot of casting calls for characters who look like me. On *Hammered*, the writers liked my audition, but they had to write a whole new character for me, to explain my face. And it worked. I got a lot of attention—even more than Arvin Mason, the guy who played Mike Hammer, the star of the whole series.

Things haven't gone so well since then.

I've gotten a lot of offers to play zombies, and they wanted me for Freddy Krueger in another reboot of *The Nightmare on Elm Street* movies. And I still get the occasional stage offer to play the Phantom in *Phantom of the Opera,* the Elephant Man, or the Child-Catcher in *Chitty Chitty Bang Bang.*

In other words, casting directors think of me whenever the role is for someone ugly who terrorizes people, especially kids. Which is not so great for the self-esteem. It's also not so great for other burn survivors or disabled people, since those roles tell people to see us as scary monsters. It's really frustrating to me that Hollywood is still making movies like *Wonder Woman* and *Us*, where the character with facial scars is evil. Movies like *Wonder*, which is about a genetic difference called Treacher Collins Syndrome, are a lot better, but they still present people like me as objects of pity.

Anyway, my agent Greg and I decided not to take any more roles like that. We started looking for better parts, roles where I could be a three-dimensional human being. I can't change the way I look, so we needed the writers to take my face into account, like on *Hammered*. Mostly, I wanted a chance to show the world that I'm more than my scars—that every disabled person is more than their disability. I had some experience after *Hammered*, and a little bit of heat, so it didn't feel like we were asking for the moon.

It turns out we were. In the last year, I've only gotten two real parts: a guest spot on *Star Trek: Discovery*, which was actually very cool, even if I only had six lines. I did the whole thing with prosthetics covering my face, so my scars weren't an issue at all.

The second thing I did was a pilot called *Freak Squad*, which is the sixty-zillionth project about a group of mutant superheroes, except in this case, we didn't have super "powers," but real mutations, or at least real disabilities. There was Flipper Girl, the Squander Twins, who were conjoined, and Melting Face Boy, played by me. The characters were all either really smart or just tried hard.

I loved the idea the second I heard it. The show seemed really subversive. The people behind it were totally cool too. I only saw a very rough cut of the pilot, but it was awesome.

But then someone on Twitter found out about it, and it became this *huge* thing, even though no one had seen it yet because it wasn't fully edited. People were furious that none of the writers was disabled, but most of the staff hadn't even been hired. And three of the actors *were* disabled, if you count me, which I do. The creators had also asked us for input on our characters and on future storylines.

But none of that mattered. On Twitter, people made the show sound like we were planning on grinding up little disabled babies on-screen. It was crazy how different the show was from what they said it was. Or maybe they would have still been upset even if they had seen it, I don't know. Honestly, they didn't seem very bright.

I really wanted someone to defend it, to say that these people were totally missing the point, that the "freak" stuff was ironic. We were reclaiming the stereotypes, and how cool was it that we didn't have superpowers, just stuff we'd learned from being disabled?

And *Freak Squad* would have been the first TV show ever with more than one disabled lead. But it was so early in the process that the network didn't even have any media people on it yet. I posted some stuff on Twitter, but then people started coming after me, saying what a monster I was. I've always gotten a lot of grief on social media, because I am sort of a celebrity and I don't look like how a lot of people think celebrities should look. But this was a new level of hatred even for me.

Within eight hours, the network pulled the plug. Because of a bunch of outraged people who had no idea what they were talking about, me and two other disabled actors were out of a job, as were the disabled writers they never even got a chance to hire.

Hey, I'm still a little bitter, okay?

In the last year, I've gone to a lot of auditions. Like, more than a hundred. I do a lot of video and Skype auditions too. And I still get my hopes up every single time. A few months ago, I was up for a remake of the old Mel Gibson movie *The Man Without a Face*. How could I not get this part? The movie is literally about a man with a burned face! The character's scars are even on his right side, like mine—I looked it up.

I didn't get the part. They went with Matthew Goode in prosthetics.

The most frustrating part of my eight years in Hollywood is that the only thing I really want is the chance to show what I can do as an actor. I've had the opportunity a couple of times on stage, and I don't think I'm fooling myself, I'm sometimes pretty good. But *Hammered* was a stupid show, and I never got a chance to do anything interesting there. And no one else in Hollywood is giving me a chance either.

That's why I'm so excited by this remake of *It's a Wonderful Life*. They want gritty? I do gritty by default. I'm already thinking about how they could adjust the character of Adult Harry to make it fit my face: I could be burned in the war, saving all those other soldiers. I'd even let them CGI the scars off my face for the scenes before the war.

"Otto Digmore?" a voice says, and I look up to see a production assistant standing in the hallway.

It's my turn to audition, and everyone is looking at me. And I realize that the smell of sour sweat is coming from me after all. So much for my Gold Bond Ultimate Comfort.

I grab my résumé and headshot, and follow the production assistant. It's been years since a producer has asked for my résumé and headshot—my agent delivers all that electronically. But it's an actor's mantra that was drummed into me back in school: even if you're certain they already have it, always bring an extra headshot and résumé to the audition with your contact information clearly spelled out at the top.

The production assistant leads me down the hallway. She's wearing flip-flops, and the rubber smacks her heels, and my three hundred dollar Testonis squeak on the linoleum. Some people dress down for auditions, trying hard to look like they're not trying too hard, but I always dress up, at least if it fits the character, trying to show my professionalism. It's not until this moment in the hallway I realize that since I've only been cast in two things in the last year, this might be a stupid strategy.

We pass a bathroom, and I wonder if I should ask to stop. I don't have to pee, but I might have to during the audition. This has never happened before. I've never had to pee during a performance either. I don't even think about things like that once I start acting, but I always worry about it beforehand anyway.

Finally, we end up in the audition room, which is exactly as bare-bones as every audition room ever. There's a folding table with three people—two women and a man—and another man behind a video camera on a tall tripod.

No one looks up or gives me any energy to draw from, but I try to engage anyway, even if it's entirely one-way.

"My name is Otto Digmore," I say, "and I've always related to the character of Harry in *It's a Wonderful Life* because I have some—*ahem*—experience with child-hood accidents."

At every audition, I always try to say something about my face right away, to give them permission to acknowledge the elephant in the room. It's not until this moment I realize that this is probably a stupid strategy too.

But to my surprise, all three of the people at the table look up. The video camera operator looks up too. They did it at the sound of my name, before my joke about childhood accidents. Now they're all making eye contact, engaging with me. Three out of four of them are even smiling.

Auditions at the big movie studios are different from the ones for, like, little indie films. The power imbalance is even greater than usual, and the casting directors all know it. So actual engagement is rare, and genuine smiles are rarer still. It's not just my joke they're smiling at now. It's me.

They were expecting me. Which makes sense since this isn't an "open call" audition. My agent specifically pitched me for this role, which means they saw my headshot, and maybe even watched my demo reel—clips of my best film and TV work. They know who I am, that I'm different from other actors, and they scheduled me anyway.

This feels like even more than that. This feels like, out of all the people auditioning for them today, they were particularly excited to see *me*.

I remember what Garlic Breath said out in the waiting room, that they're going for a gritty take.

Now I'm definitely getting my hopes up. I might have an actual chance to get this part. A role in a studio movie starring Chris Pratt.

"Do you have any questions for us?"

Casting directors always ask this, and unlike at a job interview, it's not a good idea to ask an actual question. Not unless you have, like, an actual question. Instead, it's best to get right into the reading, to let your emotions out while they're hot, before things get too logical.

"No," I say.

"All right then," the casting director says, still smiling. "Why don't we start with your first monologue? We're ready when you are." The audition called for me to prepare two monologues—one comedic, one dramatic—as well as memorize two scenes from the actual screenplay.

I nod, take a moment to center myself, and begin. My first monologue, the comedic one, is the "I Quit" scene from *(500) Days of Summer*.

No one laughs, but then people rarely laugh during auditions. The scene's not really ha-ha funny anyway.

When I'm done, I don't give them much of a chance to react before starting in on the second monologue, the dramatic one, from *King Lear*. I read the part of the Fool, the first role I ever did. I always do this for my dramatic monologue, because it feels like a role I was born to play.

It's not my best reading ever, but it's also not my worst.

When I'm done with that, the casting director says, "Thank you."

No one laughed before, and no one is smiling now, but I did just do a dramatic monologue, and two out of four of them are still making eye contact, so I'm not sure what this all means.

"Shall we read the sides?" the casting director says, and I nod.

We do two different scenes from the movie. I've memorized my parts, and the production assistant reads all the other characters in a ridiculously flat voice. I try hard to engage with her, but she gives me nothing to work with. Then again, that's pretty typical at auditions too, and is maybe even part of the challenge. To see if you can be compelling and hold the audience's attention under the worst of conditions.

When I'm done, the room falls silent again. Somewhere outside, an ambulance whines. The video operator scans his phone. I smell my own sour sweat again, and hope against hope that no one else can smell it too.

"Thank you," the casting director says, and no one is smiling, and now no one at all is making eye contact. "We really appreciate your coming in."

It's over. I'm being dismissed.

I know I'm not getting the role. They may have wanted their remake of *It's a Wonderful Life* to be gritty, but not that gritty.

Then again, maybe I just sucked.

* * *

Home for me is the basement of a duplex on Descanso Drive, right off Sunset Boulevard. It feels like it should be part of the Echo Park neighborhood, because Echo Lake Park is within walking distance, but it's actually part of Silver Lake, even though we're not anywhere near the actual Silver Lake. Which isn't a lake anyway— it's a reservoir.

Los Angeles is a confusing place in more ways than one.

I live with my boyfriend Greg, who also happens to be my agent, which is kind of a long story, but there's nothing unethical about it. It's not like he's my therapist. But it feels weird, so we try not to advertise it.

When I enter through the front door, he calls from the kitchen, "You didn't get it. I'm sorry!"

"I know!" I call back. And I'm not just saying that. I knew there was zero chance I was getting the role of Adult Harry in the remake of *It's a Wonderful Life*.

I step into the doorway of the kitchen so we don't have to shout. He's chopping vegetables for a salad, to go along with a roast chicken and some pasta salad we got at the market.

"I really thought you had a chance," he says. "They told me on the phone they were going for gritty and—"

"—I do gritty by default." I nod. "I do think they considered me. For about two seconds. I think maybe I screwed up the audition."

"I doubt that."

I step closer to him. I make sure he knows I'm right behind him, so he doesn't cut himself with the knife, then I wrap my arms around him and squeeze. Greg is a big guy, both height-wise and side to side. He's wearing gym shorts and an oversized Dodgers jersey, which is pretty typical for him. He never dresses much better, even at work, and this was hard for me to accept at first. I tried to get him to dress better for a while, but it didn't stick. But he's Native Alaskan in an industry that is very, very white, and I think that's maybe how he gets away with it. He's kind of made it his brand, that he's not your typical Hollywood agent.

Greg tips his head back, and I nuzzle him but don't kiss his neck.

"You okay?" he asks.

"I'll survive," I say.

Greg and I have been dating for almost three years, living together for two, and it's mostly very good. I used to think someone like me would never be in a relationship, and it wasn't until I started considering someone like him that I was.

Before he can ask me anything else, or smell the failure of my Gold Bond Ultimate Comfort, I pull away. I turn for the fridge to get the rest of the stuff for dinner. Our half of the house is small, and the table is a little one with only two chairs, basically blocking the back door out of the kitchen.

"Hey, you ever read a kids' book called *The Mad Scientists' Club*?" Greg asks me.

"No," I say, reaching for the deli salad, "but I love the title. And if it's about a bunch of kids who do crazy science experiments that always go wrong, I love the concept too."

"It is. Netflix is turning it into a series."

It takes all my will power to resist asking him if there's a part in it for me. I'm still an actor, after all.

"I guess the book is about seven white boys," Greg goes on. "You gotta love the sixties. But the series is going to be more diverse. I'm trying to cast Malee." This is one of his clients, a Thai girl.

I nod, still determined not to ask him if there's a part in it for me.

Greg looks over, his big brown eyes softly taking me in. It's a smile with a twist.

"What?" I say, trying to sound innocent.

"No," he says, putting me out of my misery, "there's no part in it for you."

Now I smile too. Greg really does know me well. I remember spending time with other couples before I was with Greg, and being jealous of how well they knew each other. How they teased each other about stuff exactly like this.

It feels even better than it looked.

Greg finishes the salad, and together we get the drinks, plates, and rest of the food.

We eat in silence for a minute. Then I say, "I'll clean up when we're done."

Greg nods. He knows how much I like to do chores around the house. After I had my accident as a kid, my parents tried hard to make up for it, so they never made me do any chores. When I grew up and moved away, I didn't even know how to clean a toilet—I didn't know what the brush was for—which is something that embarrasses me to this day.

"You sure you're okay?" Greg says, his eyes on me again.

"What?" I say. "Sure." But then my eyes find the tattoo on his forearm. It's on his bicep, only half visible under his sleeve: a blue and pink salmon swimming upstream. After we started dating, he told me he had no idea how he got it, that he got drunk one night as a teenager and woke up with it on his arm. He knew that his parents would be furious, so he went to his uncle for help. His uncle told him to hide the tattoo until the weekend, and then he took Greg away on a fake vision quest. They had an amazing time together—probably more profound than if they'd gone on an actual vision quest—and Greg came back and showed his parents the tattoo, and they were really proud of him. To this day, his parents still don't know the truth, and Greg is incredibly close to his uncle.

Tonight, I can't help staring at the tattoo. I can suddenly relate to that salmon, but not because it's fighting its way forward, determined to overcome incredible odds. It's the fact that it's a tattoo: stuck in place, forever fighting its way forward. No matter how hard it fights, it will never get upstream.

Before I know it, I'm fighting back tears.

Greg stops eating. "Otto? What's wrong?"

"Nothing," I say, but I'm still choked up. I put my fork down. It doesn't matter if we don't eat dinner right away, because it won't get cold. Everything was already cold.

"Tell me." He knows what I'm going to say, but he listens anyway.

"I'm so discouraged," I admit.

Greg nods.

"It's been almost three years since *Hammered*," I go on. "And nothing good ever happens."

As my agent, this is the place where Greg would give me a pep talk—tell me that something's bound to happen eventually. That he believes in me and it's only a matter of time.

But as my boyfriend, Greg is supposed to be honest with me. Besides, he's as discouraged with Hollywood as I am, and he needs to be able to talk about it too. A few years back, Greg opened his own agency, and he does okay, but only one client has ever broken out in a big way, and when she did, she promptly fired Greg and signed with CAA—one of the town's big agencies. I still have a little money left over from *Hammered*, and we have enough to pay our rent, but each of us makes less than forty thousand dollars a year. If we didn't live together, we couldn't afford Los Angeles. As it is, we can't pay for two cars.

This is the problem when your agent is also your boyfriend.

"I feel like I failed you," he says, no longer meeting my eye.

"It's *so* not you," I say, meaning it. "You're doing an amazing job. If anything, it's me."

He shakes his head hard. "It's not you. You're the best client I have, and I'm really not just saying that."

In spite of everything, I smile again. The threat of actual tears has passed, for the time being at least.

"Then the world's not ready for someone like me yet," I say, knowing he knows I mean my scars. "For either of us. All I know is that something needs to change. We can't keep going on like this."

Greg nods, but doesn't say anything else. What can he say? We've had this conversation a hundred times before, and it always comes to the same dead end.

We could try harder to get ahead. But it feels like we've already tried so hard. As hard as anyone we know, probably harder.

We could do all the gimmicky things that people in Hollywood do when no one will hire them: create a web series or put on a play. But we've already done those things too, and it didn't help.

Or we could leave town. Go somewhere and start over, do something completely different. But no matter how you dress it up, this one feels like failure. That might even be okay except it also means giving up on my dream, and acting is the only thing I've ever truly wanted to do, and it might also be the only thing I'm good at.

So Greg and I are left where we always are when we feel like this. Stuck in place like a salmon tattoo.

"Pass the dressing," I say, because there really is nothing more to say.

He does, and we eat.

Even though, inside my head, I feel like a time bomb ticking down and it's only a matter of time until I explode.

CHAPTER TWO

The following week, I meet my best friend Russel Middlebrook for lunch. It might seem kind of silly to have a best friend in your late twenties, but he and I have been through a lot together.

We met almost fifteen years ago, at a special summer camp for kids with facial scars. We were counselors for the kids, and I was one of the two counselors with scars too. Russel was there with his friends Min and Gunnar, and he ended up being the first person I ever came out to, and we even dated that summer and a little bit after. But then we drifted apart. We reconnected when he moved to Los Angeles to try to make it as a screen-writer a few years after I'd come here to make it as an actor. I still had kind of a crush on him for a while, because he's a really good guy. But he married his boy-friend Kevin two and a half years ago, and I've come to terms with the fact that we're just good friends now. Mostly. Sometimes when I jerk off, I still think about the two of us having sex, about the things we did all those years ago. But the longer it's been, the harder it is to remember exactly what it looked and felt like. That's probably for the best.

We're supposed to meet at our favorite taco truck on Santa Monica, but I'm twenty minutes late because of the traffic, and he's not there. I'm hoping he got stuck in traffic too, and when I look him up on my phone— we can track each other—I see he's right around the corner.

"Sorry!" he says, popping into view. "Sorry! Traffic. Of course."

"I just got here too," I say. There's no point in lying when he was probably tracking me too. Not that I'd lie anyway, because I'm so not that kind of guy.

We turn for the taco truck, but there's a line to order. The air smells like car exhaust and hot pavement. There's also no awning or anything, so we have to stand in direct sunlight.

"Are you wearing sunblock?" he says, shading the sun from his face with his hand. "I didn't think I'd need it. Which is stupid, since we are eating outside. And this is *Los Angeles*."

"I'm an actor," I say. "I put on sunblock before turning on the overhead light."

Russel laughs, and that makes me feel good. He has this dark red hair, which is actually kind of stunning in the sunlight. Almost shimmering. But he also has fair skin. He's from Seattle, and he's had a hard time adjusting to the California weather.

We get our food—shrimp tacos for him and jalapeño teriyaki chicken tacos for me—and find a place at a table under a plastic tarp, even if it means sitting uncomfortably close to a couple of women eating together. They pretend not to notice us—the fact that we're sitting so close, and also my scars. Everyone is good at pretending to ignore other people in Los Angeles.

Russel reaches for one of the plastic squeeze-bottles of hot sauce, which means intruding even more on the women next to us, but they continue to ignore us. Then Russel says to me, "Do you know they don't refrigerate eggs in Mexico? And do you know why?"

"No," I say. "Why?"

"Because here in America, they wash the natural protective coating off eggs, and that means bacteria can penetrate the shell. And also because we don't vaccinate chickens for salmonella. So they *need* to be refrigerated. But they don't need to be refrigerated in Mexico. Or anywhere else in the world. We're almost the only country that does it like we do. Anyway, not refrigerating your eggs is completely healthy anywhere except America."

A friend of mine once described Russel as exhausting but in a good way. It really was the perfect description of him. He's pretty animated and gets fired up a lot. But for the most part, it works.

"That's interesting," I say.

"Yeah, but when immigrants come to America, they don't always know that American eggs need to be refrigerated." He hesitates. "I just realized that sounded vaguely racist. For the record, I'm not anti-immigrant. You know that, right?" A desperate tone has crept into his voice.

I snort. Russel is only half-serious. In Los Angeles, people can be incredibly touchy about language, always eager to find fault in what other people say. It's like they want to prove how much more woke they are than everyone else. And so sometimes people roll their eyes at the ultra-woke folk behind their backs. Then again, with a president like Donald Trump, the last thing you want to do is to give aid and comfort to actual racists. That's why Russel is also half-serious.

"Did one of us get something with eggs?" I ask, a little perplexed.

"Huh? No, it's just something I read."

A moment goes by, and then I ask, "Everything okay?"

"Yeah," he says. "Why?"

I can't think of a polite way to say, "You seem even more high-strung than usual." So instead I just shrug.

Russel releases a long low sigh. "Okay, yeah. I guess I'm discouraged."

"Your writing?"

He nods. He starts eating, even though I think he forgot to put any hot sauce on his tacos.

Russel is a really good writer, but being a screen-writer in Hollywood might be even more competitive than acting. After all, every movie only has one or two writers—okay, sometimes more—but dozens of actors. Even on television, where there's a lot more oppor-tunities for writers than on feature films, a single season of a show might cast hundreds of guest actors, but they only have eight or ten writers. Then again, writers can get paid for work even if it doesn't get produced. Except for pilots, that kind of thing almost never hap-pens with actors. So far, Russel has sold one screenplay and had two other screenplays optioned, but none of them ever got made, and now they're all dead in the water. Lately, it's felt like his career is as much in the toilet as mine.

I'm not sure how honest I want to be about my own career woes, not with two women sitting next to us who could be casting directors. So instead, I say, "It's going to happen for you. It's only a matter of time. You know that."

"Lately, I'm starting to wonder," he mutters. His eyes find the bottle of hot sauce, and he remembers he didn't put any on his tacos, so he does now.

"About what?" I ask him.

Russel looks up. "Everyone always says how hard it is to make it in Hollywood, right? Because everyone wants to do what we do—write or act for a living—so the competition is insane. But if you truly have talent, and if you keep plugging away, eventually you'll break through. Yeah, it's hard, but talent and hard work eventually win out in the end. The cream rises to the top. You have to make your own luck. Put yourself somewhere so you can be in the right place at the right time."

I nod. This is *exactly* what everyone in Hollywood says. All the frickin' time.

"But what if that's all a lie?" Russel asks. "What if the game is rigged?"

I tilt my head. I'm listening closely now, very curious what he's going to say next.

"It's like this whole college admissions scandal," he says.

This is a story that's been in the news a lot lately. Rich parents, including celebrities like Felicity Huffman, have been cheating the system—paying money in order to get their teenagers into colleges that they might not otherwise deserve to attend. But I don't understand what that has to do with Hollywood in general, so I frown.

Russel leans close and says, "For years, they've been telling us that college admissions is one big meritocracy, right? That you have to *earn* your place in college, and there shouldn't be quotas, or affirmative action, or anything like that. It's supposedly all very objective. Scientific. With grades, and test scores, and recommendations, and all that. And once again, the cream rises to the top. Right? But the more we learn about college admissions, the more it turns out the game is rigged. Rich people have all these ways to cheat the system. Legacy admissions, SAT prep, and now outright lying and cheating. It turns out 'meritocracy' is just the excuse they use to keep the system exactly the way it is—exactly the way it favors the people they want it to favor."

"But what does that have to do with—?"

"Hollywood is *exactly the same thing*," he says, instantly exasperated. "They go on and on and *on* about how Hollywood is this meritocracy, and how it's all 'whoever has the best script.' 'We just want good stories!' they say over and over and *over*. But it's not true. There are all *kinds* of people in Hollywood who don't have any talent at all. How often do you see people who've made it in this town and think, 'That person is a total hack. They have absolutely no idea what they're doing.'"

"All the time," I admit.

"And how often do you see someone who *hasn't* made it, and think, 'This person is great! Why the hell can't they get a job?'"

"Also all the time."

"So if Hollywood is this pure meritocracy that everyone says it is, it sure doesn't seem to be doing a very good job."

I give a half-hearted nod. Russel has a point.

"The reality is there are all kinds of talented people—like *us*—who can't get a break," he says, "because we don't have the connections in the first place. It doesn't matter what we do because no one will read our

27

scripts, or give us a chance, because we don't know the right person, or we don't look the right way. Once again, the so-called 'rules' are just a way to shut us up. To maintain the *status quo*. Hollywood says it wants quality, but mostly it just wants to keep doing everything exactly the way they've *been* doing it, with exactly the same people in charge."

"But people do break through. It happens all the time."

"Oh, *sure*," Russel says sarcastically. "And whenever one does, they make a *huge* deal out of it, don't they? So they can preserve the myth that Hollywood is still one big meritocracy when it's clearly *not*."

Russel is sounding like a conspiracy nut, but I find myself kind of agreeing with him. When Russel first moved to Hollywood, I instructed him on all the dos and don'ts of the industry. And we did all the dos and didn't do any of the don'ts. But it didn't seem to do us any good. Now, years later, we're both eating at taco trucks because neither of us can afford actual restaurants except on very special occasions.

I start in on the last of my tacos.

"Lately, I'm starting to think that the problem isn't my writing," Russel goes on. "I think the problem is *me*. And *you*."

"Me?" I say, almost choking on my food.

"Because you and I are playing by the rules. And Hollywood doesn't work that way anymore—if it ever did. You and I are standing here, patiently waiting our turn, not making waves, thinking we'll be rewarded for that. That we'll eventually get our turn. But we *won't*. Because the rules are for suckers. Exactly like with college admissions. *They* don't have to play by the rules—the people on the inside. It's just the people on the *outside*. Which means the rules end up being just another way to keep people like you and me on the outside forever."

"You think the reason we haven't made it big in Hollywood is because we're too nice?"

Russel nods. "And nice guys finish *last*, in Hollywood and everywhere else."

"For what it's worth," I say, "the one time you did get a screenwriting job, it was because you're such a nice guy." This is true. A couple of years earlier, Russel joined me on this road trip across the country so I could audition for a role in this new movie from Julian Lockwood, the Oscar-winning director. I ended up not getting the part, mostly because he thought I was too 'different' to be a leading man. But Russel wouldn't take no for an answer. He went behind my back, brainstorming a new supporting role in the movie, one that would be perfect for me to play. Julian Lockwood didn't go for it, but Russel so impressed him that the director ended up hiring him to work on this movie he had in development. That was Russel's one studio project.

"Except the movie never got made," Russel says. "So that basically proves my point."

I think about everything Russel has said. He's not completely crazy. He's right that, if you want to make it in Hollywood in 2019, it's not enough to do good work and hope someone notices. Because no one is looking. Instead, Hollywood is giving production deals to the guy with a zillion Instagram followers, even if people only follow him because he's half naked. Or the latest web series that went viral, even if they probably manipulated the algorithms and it's a total piece of shit.

"So from now on, we need to refuse to accept the rules of Hollywood," Russel goes on, a giddy grin on his face. "We need to *rewrite* the rules. We need to reject the status quo! Be *ruthless* if the situation calls for it."

I glance over at the women sitting next to us, who are still pretending to ignore us. I lower my voice. "But what does that even mean? How do we rewrite the rules of Hollywood?"

The grin freezes on Russel's lips. Then his whole face falls. "I have absolutely no idea. But whatever the answer is, I refuse to use the expression 'life hack' or 'career hack,' because I'm already completely sick of the word 'hack.'"

I stare at him.

Then I burst out laughing. I can't help it. It's not just his joke about life hacks. Suddenly, this whole conversation seems hilarious. I mean, even if Russel is right that the secret to Hollywood success is to be ruthless and rewrite the rules, he and I are the least likely guys to ever do it. We really are Nice Guys, all the way to the bone.

Russel stares back at me for a second. Then he breaks into laughter too—so much so that the two women sitting next to us finally acknowledge us: they glare like we're a couple of idiots. Then they quickly gather their trash and leave.

Russel and I laugh harder.

Lately, neither one of us has been connecting with casting directors or script readers, but at least we're connecting with each other. And that's a really good thing.

* * *

A couple of weeks later, I have another audition, this time for a reboot of the old television series *Lost*. I never saw the first version of the show, and I don't have time to watch the whole thing, especially since I probably won't get the part. I'm reading for the role of a guy named Jesse, and he isn't established as having scars on his face, but they want to see me anyway, which I figure is a good sign. On a show like *Lost*, the backstories of the main characters are almost the whole point, and with a face like mine, the backstory practically writes itself.

The audition is taking place on the Disney lot in Burbank, and they have me on the list at the booth at the entrance to the parking garage. They give me a little badge and everything.

I park and look around.

Usually, it's fun to walk around the different studio lots. It's not like the fake "studio" amusement parks, with their attractions and crush of crowds. You see the *actual* studio, with glimpses of upcoming movies and TV shows—little pieces of scenery, people dressed up like astronauts—and you've got a badge on, so you can't help but feel insider-y and special.

But ABC-TV recently moved its offices here from Studio City, and this is the first time I've come for an audition, so I'm not exactly sure where I'm going. There are signs, but they seem to be pointing everywhere except the ABC offices. Maybe because they're still so new they haven't been painted yet. Nothing comes up on my phone either.

So I ask a security guard.

"I'm not a security guard," she says. When I still don't understand, she says, "This is a costume."

"Oh!" I say, laughing and feeling stupid at the same time.

"I know they're across a skybridge," she says. "But I don't know where the skybridge is."

"Thanks," I say, and wander on. What I really need is a map, but those only exist at the fake amusement park movie studios.

Now I'm stressed out, because I might be late to the audition. Everyone always says you should get to an audition at least an hour before your scheduled time in case you get lost or run into traffic, which is likely in Los Angeles. Excuses don't really cut it when the whole point of an audition is to make a good first impression. Besides, you also want to have some time to center yourself, because you don't want to rush in for a reading all frazzled and out-of-breath.

And I still am early—by about thirty minutes. I don't have to worry about being late, at least not yet.

Except I still don't see any skybridge, and it feels like I would if there was one nearby. So now I am worried. I suppose it's funny that I'm lost looking for the *Lost* audition, but I'm in no mood for irony.

I call Greg. I figure he'll know where I'm supposed to go.

"Across the skybridge," he says.

I grip my phone so hard I can see the whites of my knuckles.

"You don't know where the skybridge is, do you?" he asks me.

"No."

"I'll look it up on Google Earth. I can see where you are on my phone."

But as I'm standing there waiting for Greg, I hear a voice. "You're Otto Digmore."

It's a good-looking guy about my age. Clean-cut in the way that only Hollywood actors can be clean-cut, with perfectly trimmed hair and ridiculously crisp sideburns. I suddenly know for a fact that he played the lead in every musical his high school ever did. Even Tevye in *Fiddler*, if only because the director had a little crush on him.

"I loved you on *Hammered*," he goes on.

I smile, pleased. "Thanks." It's been nineteen days since anyone has mentioned that show to me. Not that I'm counting.

"Hey, you looking for the *Lost* audition? Jesse?"

I nod. "You know where the skybridge is?"

"They changed it. Didn't the guy at the front gate tell ya? It's not at the ABC offices anymore."

"What? Where is it?"

"Stage One."

I give him a blank expression, but I try hard not to be a dick about it. It's not his fault I don't know where Stage One is either.

He points—not to a soundstage, but to a nearby sign that points off to Stage One.

"Oh," I say. "Thanks." I actually like auditioning on a soundstage because the acoustics are better. I say into my phone, "Greg? Never mind. I know where to go."

As I hang up, I notice that I now only have fifteen minutes before my audition. I'm going to get there frazzled and out-of-breath whether I like it or not.

I run. It's not that many buildings away, but they're soundstages, so they're massive. You know how on TV shows set on studio lots they always drive around in golf carts? This is why.

It takes twelve minutes to get there.

And when I do, the only visible door in the whole massive building is locked.

Do I knock? What if I interrupt someone's audition?

Of course I knock. If they didn't want me to knock, they would have left the door unlocked.

I knock.

No one answers.

I knock again, louder. Have I come to the wrong entrance? They told me which lot to park in, so this seems like the closest entrance. But usually there's at least a sign taped to the door.

I knock again.

"Can I *help* you?" It's someone else dressed as a security guard. But I can tell from his expression, and the irritated tone of his voice, that this is the real deal.

"I have an audition," I say, a little impatiently. "Inside?"

"There aren't any auditions in there." Somehow, I don't know how, he manages to make his voice sound even more irritated.

"It's for the reboot of *Lost*," I say.

"That's ABC. Across the skybridge. That's not anywhere near here."

"But…" I'm about to tell him that I was told to come here. Then I remember who told me.

An actor, just like the first security guard. Except this actor was on the lot to audition for the same role as me, the part of Jesse on *Lost*. He was trying to get rid of me.

How had I not realized this right away? Was I distracted by the fact that he'd complimented my acting?

I call Greg back. "I'm late for the audition."

"What?" he says. "What happened?"

I tell him.

"You didn't really fall for that, did you?"

Is this really an audition thing? How is it that I've been acting in Hollywood for eight years and I've never heard of it? I can't help but remember what Russel said at the taco truck about how it's the guys who rewrite the rules of Hollywood, guys who are ruthless, who get ahead.

And nice guys like me who finish last.

"Let me call and explain what happened," Greg says. "I know the characters are all going to have backstories like on the old show. And with a face like yours, the backstory almost writes itself."

"Right?" I say, even though I'm pretty sure he's already hung up.

A few minutes later, he calls me back and tells me they're going to try to fit me in. He also has specific directions to the ABC building.

When I finally get there—across the frickin' sky-bridge—I really do have to pee, even if it's going to make me even later for the audition. And who do I see coming out of the bathroom but the guy with the crisp sideburns. The fact that he looks so clean-cut is another reason I didn't question him.

"Oh, hey, man," he says. "I guess I was wrong about their changing locations."

He nails the line, saying it with plausible deniability, but with the tiniest hint of mockery in his voice.

If he really did read for the part of Jesse, he's going to be tough competition, because he's clearly a good actor.

I try not to let any of this annoy me too much, because I have an audition to get through.

I manage to do my reading without completely embarrassing myself. But once again, I can tell I'm not getting the part.

Even worse, I know the guy who sent me on that wild good chase is going to get it instead. And sure enough, a couple of weeks later, I spot his picture in the trades, and I see I was right.

A couple days after my *Lost* audition, I'm at the gym when I get a text from Russel.

Can you talk? It's important!

Sure, I text back.

A second later, my phone rings, and I go out into the lobby to answer it, because I hate people who yammer away on their cellphones on the exercise machines.

"What's up?" I say.

He says, "Remember when I said that the Hollywood system doesn't work anymore, and people who play by the rules are total suckers?"

"Yeah." I still have no idea what this call is about.

"I was completely wrong!" he says, his voice squeaking a little with excitement. "One of my screenplays has been greenlit, and it's going into production. And I'm going to make sure that the system works for you too, because I wrote you the perfect part, and I'm going to make absolutely sure that you get cast in the movie!"

CHAPTER THREE

Russel's screenplay is called *Blackburn Castle*, and it's a heist movie set in the Middle Ages. An evil king has been bleeding his subjects dry for years, but the local blacksmith has finally had enough, so he gathers together a ragtag group of outcasts to steal the gold from the king's treasury. I read the script years ago, before it was even optioned, and I remember really liking it. It was such a good idea that I couldn't believe it hadn't been done before.

I'm so happy for Russel that I cut my workout short, which I never do, and I drive straight from the gym to his and Kevin's apartment. It isn't that far from Hollywood and Vine, the heart of old Hollywood. It's somehow the perfect place for Russel to live, because no one likes movies more than he does, especially old movies.

I'm also dying to know which role Russel thinks would be perfect for me. Could it be the lead? I remember his name is Benjamin Smith, because there's a joke in the script about how his job as a smith becomes his last name, and Russel told me that last names were invented during the Middle Ages, so this is supposedly the first last name ever. There's also a Chinese contortionist and an architect's daughter who's secretly an architect herself, but they're both female. And there's a thief, I think.

I knock on the door to this apartment, and Russel throws open the door right away.

"Can you *believe* it?" he says, quivering, almost tortured, like a guy transforming into a werewolf. "It's finally happening! Me! A studio movie! The budget is forty-five fucking million dollars!"

Everyone always talks movie budgets in Hollywood, and this one is pretty big. I can't help but feel a tinge of jealousy.

"I'm not surprised at all," I say. "It's a really great script." I'm not sure whether to give Russel a congratulatory hug or not, because he's not a hugger. And once again, I'm determined not to be the typical self-absorbed actor and ask about the part he thinks would be so perfect for me.

"Well, *I'm* surprised!" Russel says, turning away without a hug, leading me into his apartment. "It got optioned two years ago. Then a week after they optioned it, we learned that a heist movie set in the Middle Ages also happens to be the plot of the new *Robin Hood* reboot. So they didn't do a damn thing with it. I thought it was completely dead in the water."

I follow Russel inside. The apartment is cluttered but clean. It smells like something lemony—actual lemons, not furniture polish—and something fried.

"What changed?" I ask, taking a seat. "Why are they buying it now?" The sofa is old and dusty.

"Because *Robin Hood* came out and flopped." Russel is too excited to sit.

"It did?" It must have really flopped because I don't even remember it being released.

"It was also a complete piece of shit," Russel says. "It had that stupid cheeky, ironic tone that almost every movie has these days, but it didn't fit the story at all. Anyway, now we're back in business. Isn't Hollywood weird? Just when you think a screenplay is dead and buried, suddenly it lurches up again, like a zombie clawing its way out of the grave. And it's always the thing you least expect."

This is true for actors too. I hear stories all the time about how an actor is rejected for a part, but the casting director remembers them, and calls them for a different part six months later. Or an actor loses a role they desperately wanted, only to get an even better one a couple of weeks later—a part they couldn't have accepted if they'd taken the first one.

"Well, I'm really, really happy for you," I say. "You deserve it." I'm still determined not to ask Russel about the part, but it's getting harder and harder.

"It's already in pre-production!" Russel says, still half a werewolf. "It's so funny that this happens right after we had that conversation about how hard it is to break in. I was so convinced that the only chance I had was to somehow figure out a way to break the rules. I guess nice guys don't always finish last after all, you know?"

"Well, I couldn't be happier for you," I say again. "You totally deserve it."

"Oh! You!" he says suddenly. Finally, he sits down next to me. "You never read my rewrite, but I turned one of the characters into the perfect part for you. Dodge, the thief?"

So it is the thief. I'm relieved to hear he isn't think-ing of the lead, because I know the studio would never cast me. For one thing, I don't have enough credits to open a feature. And also, well, you know. But I might have a shot at a supporting role.

"You know how I researched the Middle Ages, right?" Russel asks.

"Yeah." That's how he knew about blacksmiths being named Smith.

"Well, it turns out that scars and facial disfigurement were really common back then, because of all the fires and accidents, and also the way people were punished. Anyway, I gave Dodge your exact scars—I even describe them in the screenplay. And the character has a *great* storyline. It ended up being my favorite part of the script."

I nod, intrigued, playing along, but I'm definitely not getting my hopes up. They're not going to cast me just because Russel described my scars in the script. For one thing, it's not like Russel has any real pull. I wonder if he can even get me an audition. In Hollywood, the writer is above-the-line, which means they're part of the creative team, not the technical one, so they have some say in the movie itself. But the writer is also the least powerful part of the above-the-line team—after the actors, the producers, and the director, who usually has the final say on everything.

"Oh!" Russel says. "I even wrote you a nude scene."

I'm suddenly very uneasy.

"What kind of nude scene?" I ask tentatively. I've never been nude on camera before. The closest was when I had to be in my underwear—a pair of boxers—for a scene in a stage adaptation of *A Clockwork Orange*, but it was the opposite of sexy.

"Don't worry, it's great, and it totally fits the script. I'm determined to turn you into a sex symbol whether you like it or not."

"I don't have the role yet," I point out. "I don't even have an audition."

"Oh, you'll get the part," Russel says, sounding utterly confident. Could he actually believe that? I doubt he's a good enough actor to pretend otherwise.

I nod once. "Okay."

"Otto? You *will*. I may have sold a script, but I'm still done playing by the rules. I mean it. One way or another, I'm getting you in this movie."

This is all just talk, and I'm pretty sure Russel knows it. But it's still nice to hear.

"Can you imagine?" he says, sitting back on the sofa, musing dreamily. "The two of us working on a film directed by Gabriel St. Pierre?"

"Gabriel St. Pierre?" He directed this buzzy indie movie called *Snark*, and it was really good.

"I know, right? And they're filming in England and—somewhere else, I can't remember what they said. How much fun would *that* be, the two of us on location together?"

Russel is getting even further ahead of himself, but I smile anyway. It really is a nice idea. Even better than being on location together would be both of us finding success at the same time.

"Wait," I say. "They're letting you onto the set? For the whole shoot?" I know it sounds funny, but the writer isn't usually on most movie sets, except for brief visits. Like I said, they're the least important part of the creative team. Plus, movie studios, which pay millions of dollars to keep the stars happy, can be notoriously cheap when it comes to spending money on anyone else.

"Well, nothing has been decided," Russel says, "but we're making the case that I'm sort of an expert on the time period." He clears his throat, making a joke. "I mean, I *am* an expert. I did three whole months of internet research. Which is why I'm scared out of my mind that these consultants they're hiring to review the script are going to find something I got wrong, and it's going to completely destroy my plot!"

I snort.

"No matter what happens," I say, "I'm really grateful you thought of me at all."

He looks over at me. "Don't be ridiculous. I know you'd do the exact same thing for me."

Would I? I think so, but so far I've never had the chance.

That night, back at my apartment, I talk to Greg about the part in Russel's movie. By now, we've both read the updated draft of the script.

"I don't really have a shot at this, do I?" I ask him. He isn't as practical as my previous agent, but he's still pretty practical, and I'm counting on him to keep my expectations in check.

To my surprise, he says, "Can I just say? I think you do."

I listen.

"Honestly, it really is the perfect part for you. The way Russel wrote it, it's like a love letter to you. I almost feel like I should be jealous."

I roll my eyes. "I hope you're not serious. There's nothing like that between Russel and me."

Greg stares at me, not even blinking. I'm pretty sure he's figured out that I used to have a big crush on

Russel, even long after we dated. But it's true what I said, that those feelings are now in the past. Mostly.

He exhales through his nose. "The bigger issue is, I'm wondering if we can finally play the 'facial scars' card."

I listen even more closely. Now I don't blink.

"It's 2019," he goes on. "It was one thing to cast an abled actor in a disabled role before—use prosthetics or CGI to make somebody look injured or burned. But these days, they can't even say, 'Well, the talent pool is too small—there are no experienced actors we could possibly cast.' Because now there's you. And you *have* experience. If that hasn't already occurred to them, I'm gonna remind them. And maybe subtly suggest that casting a non-scarred actor could end up being a problem on social media."

I remember again what Russel said, how the key to success in Hollywood is to rewrite the rules—no more Mr. Nice Guy. To be ruthless when the situation calls for it. It's ironic that Greg is thinking the same thing, but maybe that has to do with our own gloomy conversation. How both of us have no more fucks left to give.

"And then there's the fact that you and Russel are best friends, and he wrote the role specifically for you," Greg goes on. "That could make a really great media angle. I'll make sure the producers know this too. Sort of the carrot and the stick approach."

On one hand, I'm excited by everything Greg is telling me. That I really do have a shot at what is pretty much the role of the lifetime for me.

On the other hand, I'm terrified. Because with all these things going for me, that means the only way I'm not getting this part is if I somehow screw it up.

Whether it's Russel, or Greg, or both of them tag-teaming the producers together, I manage to get an audition for the role of Dodge the thief in the upcoming production of *Blackburn Castle*.

I've never been more scared in my life.

I rehearse my ass off. I work with Greg, Russel, and my acting coach. I do more rehearsing for this audition than anything I've ever done, even more than all the plays, and that's saying something because most plays are two hours long, and the combined total of time it takes to do my two monologues and the sides from Russel's script is fourteen minutes.

At some point, you can rehearse too much. You know the lines so well that they run in an endless loop in your brain, even in your sleep. You've said the words so many times, and in so many different ways, that they start to lose their meaning.

After that, all you can do is wait. And try not to panic. There's an old Hollywood expression that I focus on: eighty percent of directing is casting. Which means that the most important thing a movie director can do is pick the right actor for a role. When it comes to this role, I'm either right for it or I'm not. Weirdly, this does make me feel a little better, because it makes it seem like the decision is out of my hands. That all I have to do is show up.

But even that's easier said than done. The movie is being produced by Disney, and the audition is taking place at the offices of the movie's production company, which are located on the Disney lot—the same place I got lost on my way to the *Lost* audition.

The day of the audition, I leave so early there's absolutely no way I can get stuck in traffic, and also to give me plenty of time to find the right building, which is on the opposite side of the lot from ABC-TV. I've auditioned in this building before, at least twice, but I print out an actual hard copy of a map of the whole lot, to make absolutely sure I don't get lost again.

For the first time in the history of Los Angeles, traffic is light and the streets are wide open. So I get there two and a half hours early.

But that's okay. Better too early than too late. I park my car and work my way through the lot to the offices. In this part of the studio, everything is clearly marked, and there are even mounted maps all over the place. I still have two hours and fifteen minutes to kill, so I buy a coffee at a cart and find myself a bench in the shade to wait.

For the zillionth time, I tell myself that there's no reason to be nervous. I'm either right for the part, or I'm not. And being nervous just makes it less likely for them to see whether I'm right for the role.

But now that makes me feel more nervous, not less. Even if I'm right for the part, I could totally choke, and the producers would never know how right I am. Why hadn't I realized this before?

I try to distract myself by reading my phone, but my eyes glaze over. I don't take in anything I see. At one point, Julie Bowen walks by—she plays one of the moms on *Modern Family*, which is shot on the Disney lot—but I'm so nervous I barely glance at her.

Thirty minutes before the audition, I realize I've had too much coffee, and I have to pee. So I enter the lobby and check in, if only to use the bathroom beyond the desk.

I return to the waiting room, and I see I'm the only one there. What does it mean that there's no one else? That they're very seriously considering me, and maybe only seeing a few other actors, all at very specific times where they can give us their full attention? Or that they've already cast the role with somebody else, and this is only a courtesy read—a favor to a persistent screenwriter?

I sit and try reading my phone again, but I sat on that bench staring into the screen so long that my battery is now almost dead, and I always try to keep some charge in case of emergencies.

Fifteen minutes before the audition, I have to pee again—I definitely had too much coffee. I'm jittery too. What was I thinking, drinking an entire venti? But I'm embarrassed that the receptionist will notice that I've gone to the bathroom twice in fifteen minutes. Besides, I want to try to go right before the audition like usual.

But now I really have to pee. So I pretend to have a small coughing fit, and make a vaguely sheepish grimace at the receptionist as I head toward the bathroom, hoping she'll think I'm going there to get a drink of water or something.

I'm standing at the urinal, finishing up, when a voice says, "Otto Digmore."

I turn, but I don't recognize the guy looking at me. I'm also self-conscious because I know he's looking at the right, scarred side of my face.

He's tall and a bit gawky, boyish, but also distinguished, a little like Beto O'Rourke, the presidential candidate. His features are angular, but he's handsome enough, with white teeth and salt-and-pepper hair, stylishly cut, so thick it makes me wonder if it's all real. He's well-dressed in skinny Amiri jeans, seven hundred dollars a pair, and a blue Sartorio button-down—un-tucked of course.

"I'm Gabriel St. Pierre," he says evenly. "The direc-tor of *Blackburn Castle*?"

Oh, I think. Oh! I'm suddenly very glad I dressed up, in my Chino Guccis and an Armani button-down. Shirts made especially for being untucked have made everyone look better.

But other than that, my mind is a complete blank. I always have a little spiel to say before every audition, and I have a vague memory of having planned some-thing today. But right now he's caught me by surprise, and I can't remember what it is. I doubt it would make much sense anyway, standing in a bathroom at a urinal with my dick out.

My dick. It's not like I turned to face him or any-thing, flashing my goods. But there are no screens on the urinal, so I'm basically exposing myself to the director of *Blackburn Castle*.

At least he doesn't look down.

I quickly drop my dick back into place and adjust the elastic on my underwear, then zip up. But I've forgotten to shake, and I can already feel the pee leaking out. I hope against hope that it doesn't soak through to the front of my pants.

I turn to face Gabriel St. Pierre. Then, still flustered, I shove my fingers out for a handshake.

Which might be the single most boneheaded thing I've ever done in my life. Not only because you're never supposed to shake hands at an audition, but also be-cause he just saw me holding my dick and stuffing it into my underwear, and I still haven't washed my hands yet.

Gabriel stares down, disgusted, like I just swatted a mosquito and my blood is smeared all over my hand. Or maybe pee is even worse than blood, I don't know.

I jerk my hand back. "Sorry!" I say. "Sorry!" While Gabriel uses the urinal, I spend a long time washing my hands, and watching my face in the mirror grow redder and redder. It's the most important audition of my life, and I'm blowing it all to pieces.

Finally, Gabriel steps up to the sink next to me and starts washing his hands too. The hand soap smells like fake apples. Cloying.

Gabriel says something, but I can't hear him over the sound of two running faucets.

I turn mine off, then face him.

"Sorry?" I say.

"I said, Russel really wants you to play this part."

"Yeah?" I don't know what else to say. Did Russel mention that he and I are friends, or did he just say I was best for the part? I'm hoping only the second one, but it's probably obvious we're friends. Still, I don't want Gabriel St. Pierre thinking this is nepotism, or whatever the word is when one friend tries to get another friend a role in his movie.

I turn and dry my hands, but as I do, I realize I've splashed water onto the front of my chinos, so it looks like I've wet myself whether the pee soaked through my underwear or not. My shirt is untucked, but it was made to be untucked, so it doesn't reach far enough down that it covers all the wet spots.

Behind me, the other paper towel dispenser squeaks—Gabriel drying his hands. Finally, he says, "I'm sure he means well," and I have no idea what this means. So this is a courtesy read?

I step toward the door, then realize I've stepped right in front of Gabriel, so I jerk back, letting him go first. Gabriel leans back, unsteady, and it all comes out looking like we're doing a comedy bit in some bad stage farce.

"Sorry!" I say again. "You first, please."

As we leave, I hear a quiet burst of air, and I'm not sure if it's Gabriel making a huffing noise or just the swish of the door closing behind us.

Gabriel leads me down the hallway to a large corner office. There's enough room for a big glass desk and two white leather sofas in an L-shape facing an open area by the door.

There are three other people in the room—two men and a woman—all on the sofas. Someone is wearing Eternity by Calvin Klein.

"Look who I ran into in the bathroom," Gabriel says, but I can't read his tone.

"Otto Digmore," one of the men says, I'm not sure which, and I'm also not sure if he's answering Gabriel's question or greeting me.

I nod like a maniac to everyone in the room.

Gabriel introduces me to the woman, the casting director, and one of the men, a producer. But the name of the third man is the only one that actually reaches my brain.

"This is Aaron Sigler," Gabriel St. Pierre says. "My assistant, and also a co-producer on the project."

In Hollywood, co-producer is kind of a meaningless term, but I'm still surprised because this guy is younger than I am, twenty-five or so, and sandy blond, with a fit body. He's dressed well too, one of those Hollywood types who seem to have it all.

Including flawless skin. It's clear and smooth, like the well-stirred surface of a can of light beige paint. I stare for a moment, looking for blemishes—any blemish at all—but I don't even see any freckles or moles on his arms.

"Otto?" someone says. The casting director.

I realize I've been staring. "Yeah?"

"We just wanted to say that we've really enjoyed seeing your work," she goes on. "You're very good. We especially liked *Scarface* and *The Field*." This is a web series I did years ago, about my own life, and also a no-budget indie movie I did the year before.

"You watched my demo reel?" I say. I'm happy because casting directors don't always bother to do that.

"No, we watched the whole things. We're very impressed with you."

It takes me a second to process this. They watched my actual stuff?

This isn't a courtesy read. This is a serious audition, maybe even an I've-got-the-part-unless-I-screw-it-up read.

Except I've already screwed it up. The most important person in this room, the one I most need to impress, is Gabriel St. Pierre, and I flashed him in the bathroom, then I tried to shake his hand with a palm full of pee. And on the subject of pee, once the rest of the room gets a better look at me, they're going to think I've peed my pants. The truth is, I might really *have* peed my pants.

"Would you like to read for us?" the casting director says.

Read? Hells to the yes. Maybe I have screwed things up so far, but I still have a chance to salvage this mess. I can actually give a good audition. So good that everything up until now won't matter. Because for eight years, I've been saying that all I want is a chance to prove to Hollywood exactly what I can do. And running through my audition pieces—something I've done sixteen zillion times in the last few weeks—seems a hell of a lot easier than untangling whatever the heck Russel was talking about when he said we need to break the rules.

I move into the open area of the office. I angle myself between the sofas and Gabriel St. Pierre, who's taken the seat behind the desk. But mostly I look at Gabriel because I'm no fool.

Gabriel smiles and nods ever-so-slightly. Oh, yeah, he instantly knows when he's being paid the respect he feels he deserves. He's so tall that his eyes are right in my line-of-sight even though he's sitting and I'm standing.

Then I do my first monologue. The comedy.

And I'm good. Maybe not great, but very good.

I duck my chin, like I'm a waiter clearing the plate between the courses of a meal. Then I inhale air through my nose and start in on the piece from *King Lear*, my dramatic piece. And I know for a fact that no one is looking at the pee on the front of pants.

Because this time I'm great.

I bask in the smiles that greet me when I finish. I'm in the zone, and it feels amazing. I know it, and they all know it too. If this audition is a nut, so far I'm cracking it into a hundred pieces.

Then we read the sides—the scenes from the actual script. Aaron reads the other parts, and unlike every other audition I've even been in, he gives me something to work with. We connect.

But no one is listening to him. They're listening to me. Watching me. Because I'm still in the zone and crushing the little pieces of that nut into even smaller pieces. Grinding them into dust.

When I'm done, I look at Gabriel, right in front of me. And his is the second biggest smile in the room.

Mine is the biggest. I'm exactly that confident that I nailed this audition to the floor.

The casting director clears her throat. "So we'll be calling your agent," she says, "to schedule the screen-tests. Is that all right?"

Screen-tests. This has only happened to me twice before, with *Hammered* and *Freak Squad*. And I ended up getting both roles.

I'm almost certain I'm getting this part.

But nothing is definite until the contract is signed, and maybe not even until the cameras start rolling. I mean, screen-tests exist for a reason. And even in pre-production, the whole movie could be cancelled over-night.

Over the next few weeks, I do those screen-tests, and I also go back for two more readings with different actors. Why not? This is an important supporting role in a forty-five million dollar studio film they're casting, and they can afford to take all the time they need to get it right.

Once the whole audition process is finally officially over, I spend my every waking hour walking on egg-shells. Every time I get a text, my stomach clenches hard, and I hope against hope that it's Greg with good news. If I'm actually with Greg, I hold my breath every time he takes a call.

One day at the gym, I get a text, and my stomach clenches as usual.

But it's not from Greg. It's a Facebook Message from an old friend.

Otto! I don't know if you remember me, but my name is Mo, and we met over two years ago in Texas when you and your friend Russel gave me ride. I'm in Los Angeles, and I'm hoping we can meet for lunch.

My old friend Mo. She was a very unlikely hitchhiker Russel and I picked up on a road trip we took together. I'd been surprised, and a little disappointed, that she hadn't contacted me before now. I didn't have any way to contact her, because I hadn't even known her full name, and I'd wondered more than once if she'd sent me a message to one of my social media accounts, and I'd missed it.

I write back so fast that even Swiftkey has a hard time figuring out what I'm typing.

OF COURSE I DISMEMBER YOU!!! AND OF COURSE I WANT TO HAVE LURCH!!! HOW ABOUT TOMORROW?!?!

CHAPTER FOUR

Mo and I agree to meet the next day at a restaurant on Wilshire. It's a place I know with cheap lunch specials, and also a large outdoor courtyard that I think will be quiet. I suspect we'll have a lot to talk about.

At least I hope we do. The truth is, I only knew Mo for two days. I'd just learned her last name, which is Foster, from her Facebook message. But we had a strong connection back then, an almost instant friendship, and I've thought about her a lot over the years. I'm hoping she's thought about me too.

I get there first, and ask for a table in back, so we can have as much privacy as a restaurant allows. I sit facing the door so I can see her when she arrives.

A leaf flutters down from an old ficus tree growing right next to my table. It lands on my plate, which is white like the tablecloth, making a dry little click.

I flick it away.

When I look up again, Mo stands in the doorway, glancing around. She looks regal in a white pantsuit, which blazes in the Los Angeles sun. She's a large woman, more apple than pear-shaped, and taller than I remember. Her auburn hair is in a bun, much neater than when I knew her, and it makes her seem more relaxed, less frazzled. Weirdly, she looks younger than she did two years ago too, definitely not yet forty. But then I remember she was going through a personal crisis back then. She wasn't hitchhiking because she couldn't afford to drive. She was lost in life and looking for answers.

Her clothes make me think she's rich—I didn't know that about her either. I also don't know if she's married, or what she does for a living, or even where she lives.

I wonder again if we'll have much to talk about. If we have anything in common at all.

She still hasn't seen me, and I realize that the ficus tree must cast some kind of shadow.

I stand, and she sees me before I can even wave. Her face blooms like a daisy—her smile is easily that bright. She didn't smile much when I knew her, and I feel like I'm already seeing a side to her I didn't know.

She approaches like a train on a track, certain and unstoppable.

"Otto Digmore," she says, looming before me. Her white pantsuit is still glowing in the sunlight, and she's wearing gold jewelry—earrings, necklace, and bracelets with geometric patterns that complement each other— and they dazzle too.

I step around to pull out her chair, and she mistakes it for a hug, so it's awkward. But we end up hugging anyway, and then she waves me off and pulls out her own chair.

We both sink down into our seats, which are made of metal with hard piping in back. It feels harder and more uncomfortable than before.

"It was so nice to hear from you," I say. "It's been a long time. I was starting to think I might never see you again." As soon as I say this, I regret it because it sounds critical.

She glances at the menu next to her plate. It's Los Angeles-pretentious, embossed words on a strip of white cardboard about two inches wide and eight inches long. "I'm sorry about that. But for some reason, it didn't feel right to communicate online. I wanted to wait until I could actually see you again." It feels like there's more she wants to say, but she doesn't say it. Maybe it's not the right time yet.

"Why are you in town?" I ask. A safe enough question.

"Traveling with a friend, a sort of vacation," she says. "And…"

To see me? But she doesn't finish the sentence, just shrugs ever-so-slightly.

"So how *are* you?" she goes on. "I was so sorry to hear that *Hammered* got cancelled."

Now I shrug. "It wasn't very good."

"No," she says, eyes widening, contradicting me. She cracks a smile. "Well, okay, maybe it wasn't the best show ever, but you were really, really good. But I knew you would be. I watched the whole thing, every episode. Twice. I also watched your web series."

"*Scarface*," I say.

"Now that *was* good. Really good."

"Thanks." I can tell I'm blushing, and I hope it's not too pathetic. At least now I know she didn't forget about me.

The waiter comes and takes our drink order—a beer for me, champagne cocktail for her—but after he leaves there's kind of an awkward silence. Mo reaches for a breadstick, snaps it in half, but then stares at the two halves, not eating either one. "I'm almost afraid to ask, but I really want to know. Did you get the movie role you were auditioning for?" This was the point of the road trip that Russel and I were on—when Russel got his first studio screenwriting job.

"No," I say. "The truth is my career is kind of in the toilet right now. There's a role I might get, but probably not. It's a movie Russel wrote."

"Russel," Mo says. Her eyes twinkle like we're sharing a secret. She's the friend who called Russel exhausting but in a good way.

I laugh. "Yeah."

"Did you ever…?"

She's about to ask me if I ever told Russel the truth about my feelings for him, because she's the only person I've ever told, but I cut her off with a quick nod. "I'm with a guy named Greg. He's great. I want you to meet him if you have time."

She smiles and nods. "That would be terrific. And I'm really happy for you." She takes a bite of the longer half of the breadstick. "This role in Russel's movie. It's a big deal if you get it?"

I nod. "But that's a really big if."

"I don't believe it."

I shrug again, more impatient than I intend. I wasn't sure how meeting Mo would turn out, if it would be awkward or superficial or disappointing. Turns out it's all three.

With the bottom of her menu, she pushes the breadstick crumbs on her plate into a little line, like cocaine. I reach for a breadstick too.

"So," she says at last. "Aren't you going to ask me?"

My hand freezes, halfway to the breadstick.

When I met Mo before, the reason she was hitch-hiking was to retrace the last route of her twenty-something son before he died of a drug overdose. He hitchhiked, so she hitchhiked too, following his old check-ins on Foursquare and Facebook. The two of them hadn't had a very good relationship, and she thought that by following the route of the last days of his life, she might gain some understanding about him, or maybe just get some closure over his death. But she hadn't yet reached the spot where he died, so I didn't know what she'd learned. If anything.

She tilts her head, a little smile lodged on her lips.

I smile too. "I'm dying to know. But I didn't know how to ask."

Mo sucks her smile back into her face. Suddenly, it's like her whole being dims. Maybe it's all in my mind, but somehow the white of her pantsuit stops glowing, and even her gold jewelry darkens.

She stares off across the courtyard. "The whole trip was so strange. It was crazy that I did it, just left my friends and family and set off hitchhiking. What was I *thinking*? But I knew right away I'd made the right choice."

I forget about the breadstick and lean in, listening.

She fiddles with her menu, bending it back and forth in her hands. "I didn't tell you this at the time, but right after I left on the trip, I started seeing glimpses. Of my son."

"What kind of glimpses?"

"He used to drink this weird energy drink called M-180, and I found an old bottle in the dirt, and I was absolutely convinced it had been his. And someone carved his initials in a tree, and I was positive it was him. And I saw him in the face of someone I met." Her eyes rise, returning to mine, looking deep inside.

Me. She told me at the time that I reminded her of her dead son. That she would be so proud if he had grown up to be just like me.

I stare back, not smiling, not blushing. Listening.

"But after a while…" She stops, embarrassed. Looks down again. Puts the menu down.

"Go on. You can tell me."

She opens her mouth to speak, and the waiter returns with our drinks.

Before he can ask to take our order, I say, "Could you give us a minute?"

But the waiter has already sensed the moment between us, and he leaves without a word, just a simple bow, like an altar boy in church.

Mo gathers her thoughts, then her eyes return to me. "After a while, I started seeing *him*. Not just his face in other people, but my actual son—glimpses anyway. A silhouette off in the distance, or a shadow in the dark. At night in my motel room, I would hear his voice, but never loud enough to make out what he was saying, what he was trying to tell me. It was like he was trying to communicate with me, but we were still too far apart. But I had the feeling he was leading me onward, to the place where he died, where the barrier between the worlds would be thinner, and he'd finally be able to tell me what he needed to say." Her gaze drops. "I almost told you this at the time, but I was worried you'd think I was insane and call the cops. Or maybe I worried what it would sound like if I said it out loud, that *I'd* think I was insane."

I nod like I understand everything, because I do. "So what happened?"

"Well, I finally made it to the motel where he died, but there was someone staying in his room. I had to wait a day until it was vacant again. I was going crazy with anticipation. That night in a different room, his voice was louder than ever, but it still wasn't loud enough to make out what he was trying to tell me. I didn't sleep a wink. Then the next day, the room was empty again. And I checked in, and I waited. Listening."

Mo's story was giving me chills. "And what did you hear?" I ask breathlessly. "What did you see?"

"Nothing that first day," she whispers. "And nothing that night either."

"Then…"

"I stayed in that hotel room, day after day and night after night, and I never heard a thing. I didn't see anything more either—didn't see a shadow or hear a peep. And then finally I knew."

I stare at her. This time I don't understand.

"Eric was dead. I couldn't hear from him again because he was gone. I don't know if it was him trying to tell me that, or the universe, or just my own subconscious. But it was the truth. The only chance I had to see him again in that hotel room was if I…." Her eyes flick to one side. Guilty.

What is Mo saying? That she considered joining her dead son? Killing herself in that lonely hotel room?

Mo quickly shakes her head. "But I didn't. After four days, I closed the door on that room, and I checked out of that motel, and I didn't look back once. And since then, I've never heard Eric's voice again, or seen his silhouette off in the distance." Her eyes find me again and bore deep. "Or even seen his face on the faces of people I meet."

But there's something different about her eyes now, a brightness that surprises me. It's like she really did find a kind of peace.

"Man," I say.

"No," she says, sitting taller in her seat. Her white pantsuit glows, and her bracelets shimmer, and it's not because of the sun reappearing or anything, because there isn't a cloud in the sky. "I started on that journey looking for answers, and I found one. It wasn't the answer I wanted, but it was an answer all the same."

"Oh, my God, Mo, I'm so...."

She cocks her head, genuinely curious what I'm going to say.

"Sorry, but also happy for you. That you really did find an answer."

Her face blossoms into another smile.

"I'm sorry too, that I didn't contact you before now." Her voice sounds intense. "But I knew you'd ask me about all this, and it's like I said, I couldn't type it out. I needed to tell you in person. Because I knew you'd understand. Maybe the only person who would." Her eyes still linger on mine. "You're the only person I've ever told, and probably ever will."

I exhale like it's the first time I've ever exhaled. And at the end, I find I'm grinning like a fool. I realize how silly it was that I was worried it would be awkward between Mo and me. Okay, yeah, we hadn't spent much time together, and I didn't know all the details of her everyday life. But we'd shared an important moment in both our lives, something real, and that made us a special kind of friends.

Mo and I spend the next three hours in that restaurant, talking about everything under the sun, until the waiter turns from a respectful altar boy into a scowling librarian. Then we pay the bill and walk around the neighborhood for a few hours more, just still talking, until we absolutely have to leave, so she can get back to her friend and I can get back to my boyfriend.

We return to the restaurant for our cars. For the first time in my life, I want the valet to take forever, but of course he's back in three minutes.

"It was so great to see you, Mo," I say.

"This was a lovely afternoon," she says. "Exactly like I knew it would be."

"I'm going to text you about dinner with Greg, okay?"

She smiles and nods, and we hug, and she kisses me right on the cheek with my scars, which is the first time anyone has ever kissed me like that, including my mother. But as I turn for my car, I feel her fingers on my wrist. They're warmer than I expect.

"Otto?" she says.

I face her again.

"They say that people are the sum total of our experiences, and it's true. But what they don't say is that it's not the experiences that define us. It's the choices we make after they happen."

I'm really touched by this because I know she's talking about a lot of really personal things: the choice she made in that hotel room to carry on, her son's overdose, and also the decisions they both made before he died that kept them from having the kind of relationship she wanted.

But a small part of me wonders why she's telling me now. Does it have to do with the part in *Blackburn Castle*, which I've told her all about? But I'm either going to get the part or not, and I don't have any say in the matter, so her advice doesn't seem like it has anything to do with me.

It's rush hour, so I don't get home until almost seven, but I text Greg so he knows not to worry.

I open the door to our apartment, and I'm surprised to see Greg standing in the middle of the room, facing me. I'm even more surprised to see Russel next to him.

They both have huge smiles on their faces.

"I didn't tell you when you were on the road, because I didn't want you to get in an accident," Greg tells me. "But the producer called while you were on your way home. You got the part!"

CHAPTER FIVE

What a day *I'm* having.

Greg, Russel, and I all go out to dinner to celebrate, and Russel's husband Kevin joins us at the restaurant. This is one of the special occasions when Russel and I can both afford to eat in a nice place, not just a taco truck.

I can't help but wonder: Is this the beginning of the next stage of my life, when I can afford to eat out in real restaurants all the time? I mean, I've landed a strong supporting role that was written especially for me, in a screenplay that seems pretty darn good. And I know from Greg that I'll probably be paid somewhere in the range of three hundred thousand dollars for fifteen weeks of work, including publicity before the actual release of the film. That may not be the big paychecks that the top actors get, but it's still a lot of money.

Then again, if the movie's a flop, it might end up being the only studio feature film I ever do.

I've been waiting so long to hear if I got this part, constantly on edge, that now I can't seem to turn the feeling off. Or maybe this is a new feeling, a kind of unsettled wariness, because I remember going out to celebrate with friends after I landed my role on *Hammered*, and also after I got cast in *Freak Squad*. I thought at the time both those projects were my Big Break, but they weren't.

What if *Blackburn Castle* ends up like that too? Sometimes movies get cancelled even after they've been green-lit, and roles get recast all the time. Sure, I'd still get paid, but so what? Or what if the movie turns out to suck—if they screw up Russel's script somehow—and it ends up going straight to DVD or streaming? It might not even get released at all. Or maybe it ends up being a good movie, even a big hit, but everyone agrees I'm terrible in it, that my performance is the weakest part of the whole film, like Russell Crowe in *Les Miserables*, or Johnny Depp in everything he's done in the last fifteen years. Big stars can recover from disasters like that, but my career would be over.

At one point during dinner, Russel says, "Let's get a bottle of champagne!" and I don't want to, because I ordered champagne at all those celebration dinners before, and it now feels like kind of a curse. But I don't say anything, and we get a bottle, and we toast Russel and me, to all the great success we're going to have, on this movie and all the ones that are supposed to come after it.

That's when I remember what Mo said to me earlier that day, about how it's not our experiences that define us, but how we react to them. I have a feeling this is part of what she meant, that she's talking about friends and lovers, and trying to be in the moment. So I try very hard to do exactly that.

* * *

Pre-production on a movie is the period of time after the project has been greenlit—okayed and financed by the studio—but before the cameras start rolling. This is when the producers and the director finalize the script, scout the locations, build the sets, hire the crew, storyboard all the shots, and do everything else that needs to be done to turn a screenplay into a movie.

It's also when they audition and hire the actors. Everyone always thinks the actors are the most important part of a movie, and in a way they are. But as Russel will be quick to tell you—at length—actors usually come toward the end of the movie-making process, before the filming but after the writer and the producers have usually spent years, sometimes even a decade or more, developing the script. The leads are cast first, often before pre-production in order to nail down the financing, but the rest of the actors usually aren't cast until a few months, or even weeks, before actual production on the film begins.

In the case of *Blackburn Castle*, on the day I'm cast, we have seven weeks before the start of the production. The next day, Greg learns that the producers want to have a read-through of the script the following week. All the speaking roles will officially have been cast by then, and announced to the trades, and I'll be meeting the other actors for the first time.

The night before, Russel texts and asks if I want to drive there together.

I don't want him misunderstanding what I'm thinking, so I call him back.

"I don't think it's a good idea if we go together," I say.

"What? Why?"

"I'm a little worried the other actors might think I got the role because you and I are friends. I don't want them thinking I'm getting special treatment."

"From the *screenwriter*? You're better off being best friends with the guy who runs craft services."

Russel thinks we're best friends too? In spite of everything, this makes me smile, especially since he can't see me over the phone.

"You know what I mean," I said. "I don't want any gossip."

Russel considers this, then says, "Yeah, you're probably right."

"But I don't want you to think I'm not grateful for…"

"Otto, stop. You don't owe me a thing. All I did was help out a little with the audition. You were the one who got the job."

This is so not true. Russel also wrote the role that got me cast in a studio movie in the first place. And I have a feeling he did more than he says to get me that audition.

So I smile to myself again, grateful that I have a best friend who always seems to have my back.

The next day, I head back to the studio lot for the first read-through—my first read-through on my very first studio movie.

On one hand, I'm nervous, still worried what everyone is going to think of me, and also that I'm somehow going to screw the whole thing up. But I also can't help feeling excited. I've dreamed of something like this for years and years. Whether or not the movie goes any-where, it's still cool.

I arrive at the rehearsal room and see it's already full of people. I'm a half hour early, but I'm still the last to arrive.

So much for being excited. Now I'm just nervous.

The room has three tables lined up in a long row, with folding chairs along the sides, but no one has taken a seat yet. Everyone is standing around talking.

Like most gatherings of actors, it's mostly men, they're mostly white, and everyone is almost shockingly good-looking, even in the harsh overhead lighting. This is true even though *Blackburn Castle* is set in the Middle Ages, when people didn't have access to Botox, hair product, and muscle-isolating weight machines.

This is the way things are in Hollywood. Everything in front of the camera is supposed to look perfect, even the people. Maybe especially the people. That's why actors spend so much time obsessing about their looks, even the guys. Maybe especially the guys. Even the actors who play ordinary people on screen always know exactly how to dress and act off-screen to look as good as possible. These days, thanks to selfies, almost every person knows how to position their face to look as good as possible on camera. But actors do this in real life too.

And yeah, that includes me. I try to make the parts of me I can control look as good as possible. If that means spending hundreds of dollars on a flattering hair-cut or a decent pair of pants, so be it.

But as usual, I don't look half as good as any of the people in this room. I even see Clayton Beck, the movie's star—Benjamin Smith the blacksmith—stand-ing off to one side. He's talking to Gabriel and one of the other producers. Clayton is as close to being A-list as you can get without having the first name Chris. With his puppy dog eyes and a chin of granite, he stands out even in a room full of beautiful people.

People start to notice me. First one person does a double-take, then another. I know how it works when I walk into a room. One by one, people spot the scars on my face. I also usually know the exact moment when everyone, the entire room, is finally aware of my scars.

So I do what I always do and take charge of the moment: I step up to the closest person not in mid-conversation. It's an older man, almost ridiculously distinguished, and I'm certain he's playing the king,

"Hi, I'm Otto Digmore," I say, holding out my hand. Then, since it's polite to tell people your role, I add, "Dodge the thief."

His eyes have already latched onto my scars, but then he recovers and tries to hide it.

"Victor Bowers," he says, shaking my hand, squeezing it hard. "King Gilbert. Wonderful to meet you."

In addition to looking good, actors usually smell good too, at least when they're not sweating out their shirts at auditions for the *It's a Wonderful Life* remake. Victor's wearing Dior Homme Sport.

"I look forward to stealing your treasure," I say with a grin.

"Uneasy lies the head that wears the crown, indeed!" Victor says, pretending to huff. "Now I also have to worry about hooligans like you stealing my hard-earned treasure?"

We laugh together, but I can already tell that Victor is a pro—one of those character actors who never misses a beat, but also probably never got his real due.

I sense more people looking my way—this is the exact moment when the whole room has noticed my scars, and the very last of them are having their first look. I also see Russel, lurking near Gabriel and Clayton Beck, but looking a little lost, like he doesn't dare participate in their conversation.

I start his way. Just because we didn't ride here together doesn't mean I'm going to ignore him.

Then I see a face in the crowd I don't expect: Aaron Sigler, Gabriel St. Pierre's co-producing assistant. He's so handsome he even fits in among the buffed and polished actors. I smell Eternity by Calvin Klein again, and decide it must be his.

He catches me noticing him. An eyebrow arches.

"Well, look who's here," he says. "The screenwriter's best friend."

He says this loud enough that everyone around can hear. And almost everyone *does* hear—I can tell, because the room suddenly quiets down, like someone turned a dial on the volume of the conversation. So much for people not finding out about my connection to Russel. That makes me wonder: Why is Aaron putting me on the spot like this? Is he an asshole?

Aaron's comment gives the whole room permission to take another look at me, including Clayton and Gabriel.

I see something on the faces around me, people putting the pieces of a puzzle together in their mind.

Victor Bowers is the one who finally says what everyone is thinking. "Did your friend write that part *for* you? How interesting."

Well, I think, this is one way to make an entrance.

"Oh, leave the poor guy alone," says one of the room's few females. She steps forward from the crowd, reaching her hand out toward me. "Allison Breen."

We shake—her hand is small and warm. She's playing Felicia, the architect's daughter. She's not as big a star as Clayton, but I've always liked her. Her celebrity persona, I mean. She seems sophisticated, exactly like her character in *Blackburn Castle*. But she also looks disturbingly skinny in person, like almost every actress in Hollywood. Everyone's heard the expression that the camera adds ten pounds, and it's true, for women *and* men. But women are supposed to be skinnier to begin with, so it matters more for them. Allison also has perfect eyebrows and blindingly white teeth. I don't know women's fragrances as well as men's, but I think she's wearing Tom Ford.

"No, it's okay," I say, partly to Allison, but mostly to the rest of the room. "The truth is, the screenwriter did write the part for me. Right, Russel?" Here I gesture to the back of the room, and Russel half-shrugs, feigning guilt. At this point, I figure it's better to get it all out in the open rather than have rumors swirl around us for the rest of the shoot. I look around again, and everyone is still looking at me.

"And I totally get how unfair that sounds," I go on, "especially since I've been offered almost every other good part in Hollywood based solely on the way I look."

There's a moment of silence.

Then laughter. It's almost an explosion, so big and loud that the walls can't contain it. I'm completely surrounded by laughing faces, and I'm the focus of all this attention, but now it's the opposite of bad. This is all on my terms, people laughing with me, at my joke.

I've managed to take the thing I was most afraid of— people finding out about my connection to Russel and assuming the worst—and turn it into something amazing. For five seconds at least, I'm the most admired person in this room, maybe even more than Clayton Beck.

In the back of the room, Russel grins like an idiot. Even Gabriel is looking at me with something like respect.

I can't help glancing to see Clayton's reaction too, and yeah, his eyes are shining, and he gives me a little nod which makes me tingle all over.

Aaron is laughing too, because my joke totally landed, and he has to laugh or he'll look petty. But he's not as good an actor as me or Victor, and I can see he's faking.

Something tells me he might even be kind of pissed.

We still have a few minutes before the actual read-through, so I pull Allison aside and say, "Thanks. I appreciate your trying to help me out just now."

She gives me a wry little smile. "Oh, you didn't need *my* help. But I'm glad I gave it a shot because people like us need to stick together."

I smile and nod, but inside I'm thinking, Only in Hollywood does one of the most beautiful and successful women in the world compare herself to me. On the other hand, given the way Hollywood still writes so few good roles for women, maybe she has a point.

"Hey, have you met Ying?" Allison says, motioning another woman forward. I recognize her—she had a guest arc on *The Good Fight*, I think—but I don't know

her name. She must be playing the Chinese contortionist, because she's tiny, probably around eighty pounds,
but somehow she's still not as skinny as Allison. Even
so, her smile is enormous. If she's wearing perfume, I
can't smell it, but I can smell the mints on her breath.
Actors are always popping breath mints too.

I already really like her and Allison both.

"Hi, Ying," I say, shaking her hand too. To both of
them, I say, "I'm embarrassed that I'm just now wondering if this movie passes the Bechdel Test."

"It does," Russel says, appearing behind me. He
glances at me, his eyes still shining. Then he says to the
group, "And not in that barely-passing-so-you-can-say-
it-does kind of way."

"This is Russel, my very good friend the
screenwriter," I say, the perfect amount of hammy. I
introduce the others, and they all shake hands too.

"It's a good script," Allison says to him. "How the
fuck did you ever get anyone to produce it?"

We all laugh. Then I ask Russel, "Hey, why did you
write this script anyway? I don't think I ever asked you
that." I'm not one hundred percent certain this is a
good idea, putting him on the spot. But Russel's a smart
guy, and I'm pretty sure he can handle himself.

"I wrote it four years ago," he says. "And I wish I
could remember exactly what I was thinking at the time.
But I do know it's a story about walls—the ones we
build to lock treasure in and keep people out. And it's
also about the walls between people, the ones we build
within ourselves, to keep people from seeing who we
really are, and maybe keep us from seeing other people
clearly. And it's funny because after I wrote it, our
country spent the next three years arguing about
walls—the one Trump wants to build along the border,

but also the trade barriers between us and other countries, and the walls he likes to build between groups of people. So even though I didn't know the future, and even though the movie's set in the past, it turns out to be weirdly timely. Or maybe not. You might say that all of human history is the story of one group of people who desperately wants something fighting against another group of people who builds walls to keep them from getting it."

A couple of other people have stopped their own conversations to listen in, but only a couple. Not Gabriel, and not Clayton Beck, who's talking to what looks like his own assistant—no, two assistants. I'm totally okay with Russel being the center of attention now, not me, and even kind of proud. What Russel is saying is so obviously what the story is really about, but I couldn't have spelled it out like that. Leave it to him. That's why he's the writer, and I'm not.

"But that's all just subtext," Russel finishes. "First and foremost, I wanted to tell a good story. I mean, who doesn't love a good heist movie? And who doesn't love a movie set in the Middle Ages? I figured why not combine the two, and let's see what happens?"

Everyone smiles, and Allison says to him, "Amazing. I could tell you knew exactly what you were doing from reading the script. Now let's hope Gabriel doesn't fuck it up."

Before I can ask what she means, Gabriel himself steps up to the head of the long table. It feels like the start of something, so we drift his way. But no one sits.

"I just want to take a moment before we begin to say how excited I am about this adventure we're about to embark on," Gabriel says, his voice cracking a little. "The fact that you're here means I have put my trust in you. I can only hope that by the end of this process, I'll have earned your trust in me. Now shall we begin? I've been living with these characters on the page for a very long time, and now I'm dying to meet them in person at last."

At that, we sit and read the script.

These days, everyone has written a screenplay—Hollywood is overwhelmed by all the scripts. That's why it's so hard for screenwriters to get anyone to read what they've written. So smart writers bend over backward to make their scripts as fun and easy to read as possible. They try to grab your attention on the very first page and never let go. And Russel is a good writer. So *Blackburn Castle* is a very solid read.

But reading it to yourself in your apartment doesn't prepare you for hearing it read out loud by professional actors, all perfectly cast in the different roles. It's exactly what Gabriel said, like meeting real people for the very first time.

Out in the parking lot, Russel pulls me aside and says, "Was it my imagination or was that kind of amazing?"

"Hells to the yes!" I say. "Russel, it's a really good script."

His eyes find me in the dark. "And *you*! I *knew* you'd be perfect."

"What? No."

"*Yes!* You were absolutely great."

I smile, because secretly I think I really was pretty good.

"Otto, tell me the truth. Do you think this movie might not suck? I mean, could it actually be…good?"

I remember Allison's comment about how it'll be a good movie as long as Gabriel doesn't fuck it up.

But he gave a nice little speech, and I can't imagine what Allison said means anything at all. So I grin like the sun and say, "Your script is great, and this movie is going to be absolutely frickin' awesome."

CHAPTER SIX

The next month is a whirlwind: costume-fittings, hair and makeup tests, lighting and screen-tests with the different costumes and makeup, and also horse-riding lessons at a place called Sunset Ranch up in the Hollywood Hills. And even though my character isn't described as fit exactly, they schedule daily sessions for me with a trainer, and he takes shirtless photos of me at the end of every week and forwards them to the studio. How's that for motivation? Like I said, Hollywood wants every actor to look as good as possible in their movies, and that's true even for films set in the Middle Ages. Though, in fairness to the studio, I also have that nude scene, so I'd want to look as good as possible even if no one else gave a damn.

In between all the fittings and screen-tests and workouts, we also start rehearsals. A lot of people don't realize that movies get rehearsed like plays do. Having done that first read-through with the whole crew, Gabriel and the actors now break the story down, working on each individual scene or connected se-quence of scenes. Unlike in a play, these sequences are, at most, only a few minutes long, but it can still take a whole afternoon to rehearse those few minutes.

My first scene in the movie is also the first scene I rehearse.

We meet in the same room where we did the read-through the week before, but now there's only a single table set up with six chairs, and it's pushed off to one side, leaving a big open area. It makes everything feel off-balance.

There are four other actors in the scene, and they're already there, along with Gabriel and Aaron. Three of the actors were at the read-through the week before, because they all have at least one line, but one of the guards doesn't speak, so I've never seen him before.

Once again, I'm the last to arrive, even though I'm forty minutes early. I'm starting to think this should be the title of my memoir. And everyone's already sitting, paging through hard copies of the script. Is this a thing with studio rehearsals? Always arrive an hour early?

"Otto," Gabriel says, neither happy nor sad. Or maybe I'm imagining things. "Welcome."

"Uh, sorry I'm late," I say, taking the empty seat. I nod to the other actors, and Aaron. I introduce myself to the guy I haven't met.

Gabriel calls us to order. "Why don't we read through the sequence, start to finish?"

Thanks to Russel, everything about Dodge is pretty interesting, including his introduction. Dodge has had a hard life, because even if scars were more common back then, people were also very superstitious. They think Dodge must have been punished by God for something, and his very presence means bad luck, so everyone treats him like crap. When we first meet him in the story, a mother is so scared of him that she pulls her child away. So in order to survive, Dodge has had no choice but to turn to a life of petty crime. And he's become pretty good at it. Lately, he's been pick-pocketing people while they're peeing. Russel doesn't really describe what a public restroom in the Middle Ages looks like, so I'm really curious to see the set.

But this day, thieving doesn't go as Dodge expects. He's spotted by a local guard, and he and another guard give chase through the public market. Dodge is smart, and he stays cleverly ahead of the guards. But he's got a face they won't forget, so he needs to get out of town as fast as possible.

Then Dodge spots a third guard ahead, and ducks inside an empty building.

It's the workshop of a mirror-maker, and the thief finds himself surrounded by different looking glasses. Hand-mirrors in delicate metal settings, large wall mirrors in elaborate frames, full-length mirrors fit for a princess. They're all elegant and beautiful. And symmetrical. Nothing like the off-centered ruffian that is Dodge.

He creeps his way through the empty workshop, hoping to find a back exit. Right away, he catches sight of himself in all the different mirrors. But Dodge has seen his reflection before, and he's reminded often enough what he looks like, so he has no interest in looking closely at the scars that have caused him so much misery. Besides, there's no time to waste. He has to get out of town before the guards figure out where he went.

But halfway across the room, he catches sight of his face in one particular mirror: a folding mirror with two halves. And from Dodge's angle, the non-scarred side of his face is duplicated, so it looks like he has one whole, non-scarred face.

It almost looks…normal. Suddenly, Dodge looks like everyone else.

At this, he has to stop. Dodge has never seen this before. So he stares into the mirror, transfixed. As the actor, it's my job to communicate to the viewer what Dodge is thinking at this moment. I've decided that at first he thinks: So this is what I would look like if I hadn't had my accident. And then: So what? Why does what I look like matter so much? And then: It's not *fair*.

But lost in his thoughts, Dodge lingers too long. The burly mirror-maker steps out of the back room. Then a guard bursts in through the front door behind him.

Dodge tries to run, but now it's too late. As the guard grabs him, the mirror falls and shatters. By foolishly getting distracted, Dodge has managed to get himself caught.

In the next scene, Dodge is in jail, to be executed the following morning, but he's rescued by Benjamin Smith, who hopes the thief can help him break into the king's vault. But for the time being, we're only rehearsing the urinal, marketplace, and mirror workshop scenes.

We read through the whole sequence now, with Aaron reading the scene descriptions. I don't have any actual lines, but I act out the different reactions on my face. By now, I'm already off-book, so I don't need to look at the script for any of this.

When we're done, I'm not nervous anymore, just excited. I can tell I did a good job with my acting, because the actor who wasn't at the read-through looks like he has tears in his eyes.

"That was good," Gabriel says. "But let's do it again. And here's what I want you all to think about. The scenes in the urinal and marketplace are going to be light and fun. Dodge is a thief, and he's good at what he does—both the stealing part and the running-from-guards part. He's done this kind of thing before, and he *likes* showing up the guards. They've got a *Tom and Jerry* thing going on. But everything changes once we get inside the workshop. Those scenes in the marketplace are a set-up for the studio scene, where the tone shifts. That's where we're really going to punch the audience right in the gut."

I don't agree with everything Gabriel said. I mean, it doesn't make sense that these guards would have chased Dodge before. With a face like his, the guards would recognize him. So if they'd chased him before, they'd arrest him if they saw him again.

But that's all backstory. Who cares if the guards have chased Dodge before? If Gabriel wants to see it that way, he can. The important thing is that I completely agree that those earlier scenes are all a set up for the dramatic punch of that last scene. And I also agree that if we do it right, we'll rip the audience's hearts right out of their chests. This is the kind of moment that actors live for. It's complicated but real, which means it's satisfying to play. It will also showcase exactly what I can do as an actor, which is what I've been wanting more than anything. I, Otto Digmore, will have the audience eating right out of my hand. And the audience for a studio movie could potentially be millions of people. So I'm throbbing with energy, growing more excited by the second.

"Now *about* the scene in the mirror shop," Gabriel continues. "When Dodge catches the reflection of his face in the mirror? I want to see the yearning on his face—his all-consuming desire for a life unlived. And then I want to see his *despair*. He hates the way he looks, but there's nothing he can do about it, so he's completely defeated. This is where we punch the audience in the gut, because I want them feeling a pity for Dodge unlike anything they've ever felt before."

Suddenly, I'm not throbbing anymore. I feel like a dying light bulb. Because every single thing Gabriel said feels wrong to me.

Dodge isn't gazing at his unblemished face in yearning or a desire for a life unlived—he's gazing in anger. And the scene isn't about despair or self-hatred. Dodge might feel some of those things, but what he's mostly feeling is rage at how unfair the world is, and frustration at the utter pointlessness of it all. The way he looks shouldn't matter in the least. We don't want the audience feeling pity. That's what you feel when you see a person from the outside. We want the audience inside Dodge, understanding him, feeling his frustration and rage. We want them feeling *empathy*.

Maybe this sounds like it's not that big a deal, but it's actually the difference between acting that's cheap and sentimental, playing on fake emotions, and a performance that's complicated and real. When Dodge sees his unblemished face in the mirror is absolutely the most important moment in the whole three scenes, because it's the perfect illustration of his character, and also a pretty great introduction to him. In that one moment, we learn that what he wants more than anything in the world is for the rest of the world to see him as normal, like everyone else, but at the same time, he's convinced that can never happen, and he's pissed as hell at the unfairness of it all. That sets up his entire character arc, because by the end of the story he'll discover that he can get the acceptance he so desires, from the other thieves involved in the heist. And for Dodge, that acceptance is worth far more than any treasure they might manage to get out of the vault.

I don't say any of this. It's partly because I'm too mad. Telling a disabled actor to play on pity is a shitty thing to do.

But I'm also scared. This is my first rehearsal of my first scene in a studio movie, and I don't want to screw it up.

Gabriel talks us through the different shots. He shows us the storyboards—animated illustrations on his laptop—to show us roughly what the different sets will look like, where our different characters will be, and even the different angles he'll be using.

Then he moves us to the open area of the rehearsal room, so he can show us the blocking, which is basically the way we're supposed to move together.

"Otto?" Aaron says. "Is something wrong?"

"What?" I say, surprised. Has he seen the frustration on my face? Even if he has, he's probably trying to embarrass me like he did at the read-through.

"What is it?" Gabriel says, looking between Aaron and me. "Otto, do you have something to say?"

Now everyone is looking at me, and I feel in the spotlight, but not in the good way.

"Well…" I say, stalling for time. Do I tell him what I'm really thinking? I mean, it's the job of the director and the actor to create a character together. So Gabriel and I will have to develop a working relationship eventually. But do I really want to start out disagreeing so strongly?

"Otto?" he repeats.

"Well, I wanted to go back to the scene with the mirror for a moment. I wonder if there isn't another way we could play that."

Gabriel's eyes never leave me. "Go on."

So I do, explaining why I think the scene is more about anger than pity. I try hard not to make it sound like I'm judging his ideas, or imply that he's ableist or anything like that, because I don't want to make him defensive. Then he'll never hear what I have to say. And the fact is, he's probably just ignorant about the character. He's not necessarily bigoted.

Finally, I'm done, and I fall quiet.

Gabriel doesn't say anything.

I glance at him, but then look away, because I'm too scared of his reaction, but I do look at the other actors. They're all big, burly guys, exactly what the sequence calls for. But they're also professional actors, so I know they're sensitive types no matter how butch they look because emotions are literally what we actors do for a living. Two of them are smiling, and one of them even gives me a little nod, which tells me they both understand and agree with everything I had to say. The other two guys keep their faces blank, but they meet my gaze, and I'm pretty sure they agree with me too, but don't want to risk alienating the director and lose out on a cushy studio gig.

Did I alienate the director? Did I make a big mistake by speaking up?

Finally, I dare a look at Gabriel, but his face is blank too. I have absolutely no idea what's going on inside his head.

But I know what's going on in mine, which is me freaking out, thinking: Please, please, please let him not fire me.

Then, finally, Gabriel shrugs and says, "Maybe you're right. You probably know more about the character than I do. Why don't we try it your way?"

Some directors are nurturing, creating an emotional bond with their actors, an environment of total trust right from the start. That way they're able to tell the actors uncomfortable truths in an atmosphere of love and support. These directors have a way telling you exactly what you most need to hear, at exactly the moment when you most need to hear it.

Other directors are more disciplinarian, like a hard-ass sports coach. These directors are harder on their actors, and much less supportive. At times they might be distant or even outright cold with you. This can be tough in the moment, but at some point, you realize it's part of a long-term strategy. They're being distant with you because they want your character to feel lost. Or they're hyper-critical because they want you to find your character's anger. Once you make the breakthrough, you end up being grateful that the director helped you access some difficult part of the character that couldn't otherwise reach on your own.

Then there's Gabriel St. Pierre.

He isn't either kind of director. He doesn't seem to have much strategy at all. In the days of rehearsal that follow, I learn his direction is all obvious, surface stuff. He directs us like we're doing a television movie: really broad and simple, everything underlined so no one could ever possibly miss it. He doesn't even try to look beyond the scene, to see what's going on under the surface.

Which is a problem because the director is supposed to be the one with the vision, the person who understands the story more than anyone. A good director knows how everything fits together, and how every little thing serves the overall movie. He's the one who makes everyone else's choices make sense—not just the actors, but the set and costume designers, the director of photography, the light and sound technicians, even the guy who knocks the clapperboard together. Every single person involved with the movie.

If Gabriel has a vision, I can't see it.

Then again, maybe he doesn't need a vision, because Russel's screenplay is good. If he just films the thing the way Russel wrote it, maybe it'll still end up an okay movie.

Two weeks after rehearsals begin, we're rehearsing again, a flirty, subtext-y scene between Benjamin and Felicia in Benjamin's workshop. Benjamin is explaining the forging process to Felicia, talking about anvils and tongs and bellows, and the process that makes things hotter and harder. Except he's really talking about the physical attraction between him and Felicia. It's clever dialogue, more than just sex puns. My character is outside, and overhears through a window, and then Dodge stares across the marketplace at Mika, as if he's wondering if any woman will ever see him the way Benjamin and Felicia are starting to see each other.

"More!" Gabriel directs me at one point. "When you look at Mika, you have stars in your eyes. She's everything you want a woman to be!"

Which is terrible direction. When Dodge looks at Mika, he doesn't have stars in his eyes. He has longing, yes, but also pain and fear and resentment, and also lust because I've already decided that Dodge is a twenty-nine year-old virgin. He went to a brothel once as a teenager, and the women all looked horrified that he might touch them, so he left and never went back.

Before long, we break for lunch.

By now, I've learned that Clayton Beck never goes anywhere without a slightly rotating entourage of at least three people. They wait in the hallway while we rehearse. They must also listen at the door because the second Gabriel calls for lunch, they appear and whisk Clayton off to see and be seen at one of the crazy-expensive bistros right outside the lot. I'm a little disappointed because I'd hoped he and I might go to lunch together. By this point, I've only said a grand total of eight sentences to Clayton, not counting scenes where our characters have talked. Even in real life, he has that perfect movie star drawl.

But Allison doesn't have an entourage, and she asks me if I want to grab a bite.

"I'd love to," I say, and we end up getting sandwiches at one of the commissaries, then searching for a place to eat outside. Along the way, we talk about our different pasts, and I learn that her sophistication is a conscious choice: a public identity she made up. She's really a small town girl from Alabama.

"You don't have an accent," I say.

"Lost that before I lost my virginity," she says proudly, also revealing her twang.

I feel stupid I hadn't considered that her sophistication was all an act. People in Hollywood are famous for reinventing themselves. I never cared about the way I dressed until I moved here.

We find a bench to eat, and I say, "Hey, what did you mean the other day when you said that the movie will be good if Gabriel doesn't screw it up?" I've been meaning to ask her this for a while.

She takes a huge bite of her sandwich and talks with her mouth full. "What?"

"The day of the first read-through," I say.

She swallows and thinks for a second. "Just something I heard. Why? What do you think of him so far?"

I have an opinion, but I'm not sure I want to say it out loud in case it gets back to him.

"Come on," she says. "Just say it." She has mustard on her lips, and also a little smirk.

I laugh. "Okay, I'm not very impressed. But—"

"—you're still hoping it might be a strategy to get something out of you? Yeah, sorry, no, I think he really is that thick. 'When you look at her, you've got *stars* in your eyes.' Ha!"

"Are you saying he's a bad director?"

"Sure as hell seems that way."

"*Snark* was good." This is the last movie he directed.

"I heard they saved it in editing. And he had a good DP—like, *really* good. Who Gabriel fought every step of the way." The DP is the director of photography, also known as the cinematographer. The guy who controls how the movie looks.

"Maybe that will happen this time too."

"Maybe," she says, but it's clear she doesn't believe it.

"So what are you saying? You think the movie's going to suck?"

"Oh, anything can suck. Who the fuck knows?"

"You're not worried?"

She takes another bite right before she speaks, talking with her mouth full again. I like that she already feels like she can be her real self around me. That she doesn't need to pretend to be a dainty sophisticate like she's on *The Tonight Show with Jimmy Fallon*.

"I'm always worried," she says. "But there's nothing I can do about the movie itself. The only thing I control is my own performance. So when a director is bad, I use a strategy. Then even if the movie's a piece of shit, I don't embarrass myself."

"What kind of strategy?"

She swallows and thinks for a second. "You're gay, right?"

I'm surprised but try not to act offended or anything. "Uh, how did you know…?"

"Good gaydar. So if you're gay, you know the difference between a bossy bottom and a power bottom."

"I do?" Now I'm even more surprised. What is Allison talking about? Why did she bring this up?

"Don't you?" she goes on.

"Let's say I don't."

"Well, both a bossy bottom and a power bottom are when the bottom is in control of the fuck, right? Not the top, which is more typical. A bossy bottom is what it sounds like: someone who fusses and complains, and is just generally difficult to be around. High maintenance. In the end, it's going to be a bad fuck—for the top, but also for the bottom."

I laugh because I don't know what else to do. "Okay."

"But a *power* bottom is when the bottom takes control, but it ends up being a *good* fuck. So how does he do that? He's in charge, but he works *with* the top. He doesn't bitch and complain. He might figure out what the top wants, and then use that to guide the top to do what the bottom wants. Or he might *dominate* the top, forcing him to satisfy the bottom's needs, but in such a way that it totally gets the top off too. Basically, rather than ignore the top, treating him like he's a dildo or a blow-up doll, he gets inside the top's head, working with his desires, opening him up and getting him to a place where the bottom is totally in control."

I'm trying very hard not to blush. And failing.

"This is all very interesting," I say. "But what does it have to do with what we were talking about?" I'm also wondering how she knows so much about gay male sex, although even as I think this, I realize that maybe heterosexuals have a "top" and a "bottom" in their sex too, and it's not necessarily the man who's the top. I've never had sex with a woman.

"Well, it's exactly the same dynamic for an actor and director," Allison explains. "The director is the top, obviously, and the actor is the bottom—again, obviously. And usually the director is in control, just like in sex. But if it's a bad director, the *actor* needs to take control, because otherwise you end up with a bad performance. But you can't be a *bossy* bottom, because you'll still end up with a bad show. So you need to be a *power* bottom. You need to take control of your own performance, but do it in such a way that the director is on board, and loves you for taking charge."

I think about all this. Her description of sex isn't anything like the sex I've had in my life. But apart from the actual "sex" thing, she's making a certain kind of sense. It's a good metaphor or whatever.

I burst out laughing.

"What?" Allison says, gauging me with a smile.

"That might be the smartest thing I've ever heard about the actor-director relationship in my entire life."

"Right? It's spot-on, isn't it? I want to write it up and post it somewhere, but I can't do it under my real name."

"So you and I need to power-bottom our way to good performances? Turn Gabriel into our little bitch?"

"*Now* you've got it." She gives me a kind of "Cheers!" with her Diet Sprite, then takes a swig.

"Because otherwise we're both gonna be screwed," I say, "and not in the good way."

Allison laughs, squirting Diet Sprite out of her nose and onto her blouse, and that makes us both laugh harder.

I liked Allison before, but now I *really* like her.

I also feel a little burst of optimism about the movie. Power bottom? I can do this. The more I think about it, the more I realize I might have *some* idea what she's talking about even in actual sex.

CHAPTER SEVEN

Four weeks later, rehearsals are over, and it's time to fly to England to start shooting the actual movie. But it won't be shot in chronological order. Almost every movie you've ever seen was shot completely out of order.

This might seem a little strange at first, but it makes sense when you think about it. Most stage plays are either set in a small number of locations, or in a lot of locations that are only minimally suggested, with sets that can be swapped out really fast. But most movies take place in lots of different locations with a lot of different sets, and those sets are way more detailed. They're complicated and expensive to make.

So from a technical point of view, it makes sense to film all the scenes in any one location at the same time, all in a row. That way, the producers only have to set up all the heavy cameras and lights and equipment once. It's cheaper too because they can rent the soundstage or location for a shorter period of time. So most movies shoot *all* the scenes that take place in one particular location, no matter where they happen in the script, and then they move on to the next location.

Like Russel said, we're shooting exteriors in England, in the actual Sherwood Forest from the legend of Robin Hood. It's now a big public park, and it looks like England in the Middle Ages. Or at least what everyone thinks England looked like back then. Why do we think that? Because every movie set in the Middle Ages is shot in the Sherwood Forest park, or in another British forest that looks exactly like it.

It's weird how movies mirror reality even as they're also shaping it. Russel would probably have something really interesting to say about that.

One good thing is that since Russel and I have been outed as friends, there's no reason we can't fly to England together. But when I call the airline to see about getting us side by side seats, I find out that the studio has put me in first class and Russel back in coach. I wish I could say I'm surprised, but I'm not. Without telling him, I pay the difference for an upgrade so we can sit together. Then I text him to say we all had screw-ups with our tickets, and he's being sent a replacement one.

The day of the flight, we get to the boarding area, and I realize that Allison and Clayton Beck are on our same plane. But Clayton is traveling with an entourage of five people, and I'm not sure he even notices us. And Allison is wearing big dark glasses like she's hung over, so we don't talk to her either.

I feel Russel looking at me.

"What?" I say.

"We're about to board a plane to fly to England," he says.

"I know."

"So *you* can act in a movie that *I* wrote."

"I know."

"A *real* movie. A studio movie. Starring Clayton Beck and Allison Breen."

"I know."

For a second, we both stand there grinning like idiots. Then Allison burps so loudly it echoes all the way across the waiting area.

It's all we can do to keep from busting up.

Later, on the plane, after we're settled in and buckled up, Russel asks me, "So. How'd you feel about rehearsals? What do you think of Gabriel as a director?"

Russel has been asking me different versions of this question for five weeks now, ever since rehearsals began. And before now, I always found a way to change the subject, or say something vague that implies Gabriel is a much better director than he really is. But a lot of those ways involved me being too busy to go into too much detail. I was trying to give Gabriel the benefit of the doubt, waiting to see if maybe he did have some kind of strategy.

Now there is no doubt. After five weeks of rehearsal, I know he's a disappointing director. During rehearsals, I did the best I could, trying to be a power bottom to his hopeless top, like Allison said. But it turns out that's easier said than done. Or maybe I'm just a lousy bottom, I don't know.

Somehow I need to tell him what I've learned. Well, not the part about being a lousy power bottom, but the rest of it, that Gabriel really could screw up this movie. For one thing, we've just sat down on a flight to England, and I can't keep changing the subject for eleven hours. But more than that, Russel is my friend, the guy who made all this happen in the first place. It feels like I owe him the truth.

"Well…" I say.

Russel instantly looks stricken. "That bad?" He lets his head fall back against the headrest. "I had a feeling."

I should have known Russel suspected.

"He's going to ruin it, isn't he?" Russel laments. "The whole movie."

"Russel, no," I say quickly. "It's not what you think." This movie is a big deal to him—it's a big deal to *me*. I want to tell the truth but in a way that doesn't completely crush his dreams.

Russel stares at me—hopeful, waiting. But I can't think of any way to soften the blow.

Finally, I say, "It wasn't entirely bad. Gabriel did *some* things right. And he didn't screw up *every* scene we rehearsed."

"Oh, great, he didn't screw up *every* scene." Russel raises his hand, trying to get the attention of the flight attendant, probably so she can bring him a drink despite it being nine-thirty in the morning.

"There are different kinds of directors," I go on. "Some directors are actors' directors—the ones who are really good working with actors. For them, the most important thing is the performances, the emotional stuff. They care about the other things, the shots, the 'look' of the movie, but that's not as important as the performances. They leave that to the DP."

"I *know* what an actors' director is," Russel says, a little sullen.

"Okay, okay. Well, so maybe Gabriel's not an actors' director. That means he's probably a technical director."

Russel looks at me warily.

I go on. "That's the kind of director who's good with the technical side of things. They know shots and angles, and they're obsessed with the actual 'look' of the film, every little detail. And maybe these directors aren't so good with actors because they either don't care, or they aren't very good with people in general. But that doesn't matter, because there's usually someone else around who helps out with the performances—the assistant director or even the writer. And with *Blackburn Castle*, maybe you *want* a technical director because the script is already so solid. The characters already make sense, so the actors can figure most of it out ourselves. And when we get off track, you'll be there to straighten us out. So then Gabriel can concentrate on making the movie look as fantastic as possible."

"I know what a technical director is too," Russel says, even more sullen. But I notice that when the flight attendant arrives, he orders a coffee, not a Bloody Mary, so I'm pretty sure I'm getting through to him. And what I'm saying *is* all true. I'm proud I came up with all that on the fly.

I tell the flight attendant I don't want anything.

When she leaves, I shift in my seat so I'm facing Russel full-on.

"It's going to be okay," I say. "I should have led with this, but the other actors? They're fantastic. I mean, really, really good. And you know the old adage, that directing is eighty percent casting."

Russel nods, and I'm also proud I remembered to add this. Casting really is the most important thing a director does, and the actors Gabriel chose truly are good.

I take his silence as an opportunity to add, "Gabriel can't be too terrible a director if he got the casting so right. Right?"

Russel sighs. "I guess you're right."

"I *know* I am."

He smiles at last. And I feel really good that I was able to cheer him up.

But when the flight attendant returns with Russel's coffee, I tell her I've changed my mind and that maybe I'll have a Bloody Mary after all.

When we land in Heathrow airport in London, it's morning the following day. Or maybe it's morning the day before. I've completely lost track of time, and I'm too tired even to check my phone. All I know is that it's basically evening my time, and I want to go to bed. But rather than stay in the city, the studio has arranged transportation for us to go directly to where we're staying near Sherwood Forest, which is about a hundred and fifty miles from London, or two hundred and fifty kilometers. So I won't be sleeping any time soon.

Once we're cleared customs and immigration, I meet a limo driver holding a sign with my name on it. Allison and Clayton have their own drivers too, and I think Clayton has a separate limousine for his entourage, which came with him all the way from Los Angeles.

I look around for a sign with Russel's name on it.

He sees me looking and scoffs. "I'm in one of the vans with the crew."

Russel's not kidding when he talks about how badly they treat screenwriters in Hollywood.

"I know," he says, reading my face. "I'm surprised too, especially after they sprang for first class."

I'm suddenly fascinated by the floor, which is made of some kind of ceramic tile.

"Wait," Russel says, his eyes boring into me like a laser. "Otto, you paid for my upgrade, didn't you?"

I ignore the accusation. "Why don't you ride with me? I'm sure there'll be plenty of room." I look at my driver, who shrugs but in a weirdly British way. Stiff.

"That depends," Russel says. "Where are you staying?"

I'm embarrassed to admit that I'm staying in a place called Thoresby Hall, which is this beautiful old mansion that's been converted into a hotel. It's like something out of *Downton Abbey*, but I'm suddenly sure it's only the leading actors who are staying there, along with Gabriel and maybe Aaron. The rest of the cast and crew—and Russel—have no doubt been booked in cheap guest houses.

"Let's just go," I say. "We'll figure everything else when we get there."

Russel refuses to let me rent him a room at Thoresby Hall, which is probably just as well since it's four hundred dollars a night, and that would add up fast. But I'm glad I make the offer. I have my driver take Russel to his guest house.

I stay up long enough to call Greg and tell him I survived the flight okay. I also get an early dinner. Then I go right to bed, despite the fact that they say the quickest way to adjust to a new time zone is to go to bed at your "normal" time.

But who cares if I wake up at two in the morning? That just means I'll be able to work out before my six a.m. call-time.

We'll be in England for a grand total of eighteen days. Most of our time will be in different locations in Sherwood Forest, but we'll also be spending four days shooting exteriors at a place called Shirell Castle, which isn't open to the public but still looks familiar to people because it's been in a lot of movies. It's well-preserved, but they'll use subtle CGI to make it look even newer in our film.

I'm hoping Russel and I get a chance to go into Nottingham at some point since it's only twenty kilometers away. I'm sure it's all touristy and kitschy, nothing at all like the actual *Robin Hood* stories, but if I'm being honest, that's part of the appeal.

The next day, I'm on location in Sherwood Forest at six a.m., and I feel pretty good, sleep-wise. But I'm way more nervous than I expected to be, even more than I was before my first audition.

Weirdly, the very first scene we're shooting is the last scene in the movie.

Shooting movies out of order might make sense for the producers, but it's very weird for the actors. Sometimes you're watching a movie, and something incredibly traumatic happens to a character, like someone else dies or something, and in the very next scene the character seems fine. That might be because everyone's trying to keep the story moving. But it could also be because the scenes were filmed out of order. The actors read the whole script, and usually rehearse it too, but it's hard to keep it all straight in your head. Emotionally, I mean. You think: "What is my character feeling at this point again?" Also, no performance is ever truly "real" until you perform it in front of an audience or camera. A big part of any performance is finding the unexpected moments in each scene—things that feel real at the time. But once it's shot, it's locked into place. And if you're filming the movie out of order, you can be forced to make choices for earlier scenes that you might not truly understand until later.

It's all very complicated. First and foremost, you want your character's emotional journey to look real, the way an actual person would react under those circumstances. But that's hard to do when the actor's experience is so different from the character's one.

Back in Los Angeles, I was glad we were filming the exteriors first. In this movie, most of the complicated scenes take place indoors. By doing the easy stuff first, I figured we could sort of ease our way into the characters.

But now that we're in England, I learn that the first scene we're filming is the last scene in the movie, and it's not an easy scene at all. And that has me back to thinking Gabriel St. Pierre is definitely not an actors' director.

Spoiler alert: by the end of *Blackburn Castle*, the little band of thieves does manage to steal the gold from the king's treasury. And in the final scene, we all meet in this hidden little clearing in the woods, and we're dividing the treasure up into equal parts, loading it into the saddle bags on our different horses. We know we can't ever go back to the castle, because the guards will recognize us, especially me, so we're setting off for parts unknown. And since it was a one-time score, and now the job is done, we're all heading in different directions.

But the subtext of the scene is that nobody really wants to split up. Part of it is that Mika, the Chinese contortionist, is attracted to Dodge, who loves her back but isn't used to the attention of a woman. Benjamin

Smith and Felicia have romantic feelings too. The fifth thief is an old magician/con artist named Gordo the Magnificent who just wanted to pull off one last big swindle before he died. Or so he thought. He's since learned that what he really wants is to be part of a family again.

Throughout the heist, the five of us have come to like and accept each other exactly the way we are. Five wary, desperate loners have become a family of sorts. And we're all reluctant to give that up. But we're also all used to being disappointed and rejected, so no one wants to say that outright.

So one by one, as we're packing our bags, we all make up excuses to travel in the same direction. To stay together a little while longer.

And then we ride off into the trees as one, and it's clear we won't be breaking up any time soon. We all finally have the treasure we so desperately wanted, and it isn't the gold in our saddlebags.

Russel has written a really sweet scene—the perfect ending to the story. But it's really weird to be acting all these emotions of love and longing as a character who, from my point of view, hasn't really done anything yet. Rehearsals aren't the same thing as the performance.

That's why I'm so nervous.

I can't tell if the other actors feel the same way or not. They all have a lot more experience in feature films. But whatever they're thinking, I need to get a grip. Because this is one of, like, three scenes in the whole movie when my character isn't especially nervous.

On most movie sets, they shoot the same scene over and over again, from different angles—first, wide angle, often from different positions, then close-ups on all the characters. They do every shot until the director feels absolutely sure he got the right one. Then they do it again, just in case something is wrong and they don't notice it in the moment. Or maybe the director wants different choices when he gets together with the editor, to assemble the different shots into a finished film.

We all take our marks and start in on the scene, doing the first take, and I'm still pretty nervous. But we rehearsed this scene back in Los Angeles. For once, Gabriel didn't have any particularly stupid ideas. He and the actors were all more or less on the same page. So once the cameras start rolling, it doesn't feel as strange as I'm expecting. Our marks are identified with tape or rocks on the ground, and the blocking all comes right back to me.

Then I'm in the moment. As the scene progresses, I give what feels like a particularly good look to Mika, a hint of an actual romance to come. I hope I can duplicate it when it comes time for my close-up.

After that first take, Gabriel calls, "Cut!" which means the cameras stop rolling, and the actors are supposed to stop acting.

I look over at Russel, lurking in the background, behind all the assistants and technicians. I said before that whenever you get a group of actors together, they're mostly men, and white, and incredibly handsome, with clothes and haircuts that are as flattering as humanly possible. The crew is the same in some ways: also usually men, and also mostly white. But they tend to be out of shape, and pay less attention to their hair and clothes. There are a lot of bald heads, and oversized glasses with greasy lenses, and bushy beards.

So Russel would stand out anyway. But right now, he looks like a mother dog with new puppies, proudly surveying the scene, watching his characters finally come to life.

Gabriel huddles with the DP and some of the other crew, to talk about how things look so far. These days, movies are almost all shot digitally, not on actual film, and they're watching the playback on a monitor. It hasn't been color-corrected, which is when the picture is made more vivid in editing, but they can at least see if they're in the ballpark.

As they talk, the other actors and I wait. Allison and Ying chat, and the actor playing Gordo reads his phone. Technically, you're not supposed to have phones on movie sets, because people forget to put them in air-plane mode, but this rule is almost never enforced. I still really want to talk with Clayton Beck—by now, I've spoken thirteen whole sentences to him—but his en-tourage is with him on the set too, and they've got him surrounded again.

Because Gabriel and the crew are mostly men, they talk loudly. I eavesdrop.

"We can't do that shot without adding another setup of Mika to bridge them," the DP is saying.

Gabriel asks why.

"Because it crosses the line and you'll be screwed in the editing room," the DP says.

"Crosses a line?" Gabriel asks.

"Not *a* line—"

"Oh, right, *the* line. The axis of action, yeah, I know that. Let's do that then. Also, I'm worried about these shadows. Can we adjust the key? I mean the fill."

At this, it's all the DP can do not to roll his eyes. It sounds like Gabriel barely has any idea what he's talking about.

I remember what I told Russel on the plane, that Gabriel isn't an actors' director, but that meant he was probably a technical one. It hadn't occurred to me that he might not be either.

So what's the third option? That he's a bad director? Or maybe just a mediocre one. But how is that possible? Why would the studio hire someone like that to direct a forty-five million dollar movie?

My eyes return to Russel, back behind the crew. He doesn't look quite so proud anymore—now he's more like a mother dog whose puppies have died. He overheard everything I did and probably came to the same conclusion.

But suddenly I have other problems to worry about.

In every TV or film production, there's something known as a call sheet, which shows what scenes are being filmed, when and where—and more importantly, what actors are needed.

Right then, a production assistant hands me the call sheet for the following day.

And I see that our second day of filming is going to be my nude scene.

CHAPTER EIGHT

My nude scene seems simple enough. It's me bathing in a stream, and then Mika comes along and sees, and I see her seeing me, and we have a moment. But there's actually a lot going on. There's a lot going on behind-the-scenes too, like what it means for a guy like me to do a nude scene in a major motion picture.

The next day, alone in my trailer before the shoot, I think it over.

On one hand, I'm scared again. It sucks that Gabriel and the producers scheduled two of my most difficult scenes for the first two days of production. I mean, getting naked on camera is strange for anyone, but especially for me. It'll be a closed set, which means it'll just be the essential technical crew, and Russel, since I want him to be there. But that's still dozens of people, and they'll all be seeing me naked for at least four hours, because that's how long it takes to do multiple takes of even the simplest scene.

Then there's the fact that once the movie is released, *everyone* will see me naked. Everyone I've ever met, if they want to look, and also lots of people I haven't met. Basically, anyone in the entire world who wants to know what I look like naked will be able to watch the movie. Or even look up stills of me online, since there are whole websites that do nothing but take screen captures of anyone who's ever been naked in a movie or on a TV show. (How do some people live with themselves?)

And I'm going to be *completely* naked. They'll be able to see everything. According to Russel, that's the whole point of the scene—my character being totally vulnerable, and also an object of beauty to Mika, because she, like the viewer, isn't necessarily expecting someone like me to be something like that.

But the thing is, I'm not *that* scared. This is only the second day of shooting, and I was definitely expecting to be terrified. So I wonder why I'm not.

For one thing, it *is* a simple scene, so it'll be hard for Gabriel to screw it up. Also, I completely trust Russel. I know what he's doing with this scene, and I'm totally on board. Turning me, Otto Digmore, into a sex symbol? Russel called it subversive, and I don't think he meant it in an insulting way. I mean, it's just a fact: not very many people have ever wanted to see me naked. And I used to be kind of a celebrity, and everyone loves seeing celebrities naked. It's like how no journalist has ever asked me if I'm gay, and no gossip blog has ever spread the rumor that I am, even though I'm completely out in my personal life. Because people don't see someone like me as a sexual being. They don't *care* if someone like me is a sexual being, because it's not a turn-on for them.

But now maybe it will be.

The scene is also a really important part of my character's arc. Dodge realizes, maybe for the first time in his life, that not everyone sees him as an ugly outcast.

That Mika wants to see him naked, and she likes what she sees. And that makes Dodge start to see himself differently. He realizes that maybe he's not doomed to be an outcast forever, at least not in everyone's eyes.

Like I said, there's a lot going on. The scene, like the whole character, is a thing of beauty.

They haven't called me to set yet, so I stand in front of the mirror in my trailer, and I take off my robe and look at myself, at my naked body. Obviously, I've seen myself in the mirror before.

But it's been a long time since I've really looked.

The first thing I see is the scars on my face that run down onto my shoulder and under my collar bone. It's basically all one scar, but it looks different on my body because I had less plastic surgery there. It's mottled and shinier. A little lumpy. No one's ever seen these scars on my body before—the general public, I mean. I wore a t-shirt when I was in my underwear for that stage production of *A Clockwork Orange*. And I once did a shirtless beefcake photo shoot for charity, but I made a point to keep the scarred part of my body turned away from the camera. I guess I was embarrassed people would see that I'm even more damaged than they knew.

I'm not embarrassed now.

I work out a lot, and my whole body is pretty lean and fit. I look at my shoulders and arms, and I see that I've built up some decent definition, even under the scars. My chest is pretty well proportioned. I don't have washboard abs, but I have the start of abs—the suggestion of abs—especially if I flex a little. There's a little bit of hair on my chest, even if it's a little asymmetrical, because there's no hair on the scarred part. It's darker than the hair on my head, and a trail leads down to my crotch where it's darker still. Some guys trim their chest hair, but I've never had to. They told me not to trim anything anyway. They wanted me to keep my body hair as natural as possible.

When that word came down to me, I had just trimmed the hair around my cock, and also shaved my balls. This was only five weeks ago, so the woman who did my body makeup earlier that morning took one look at me and said, "Nice! But I wonder how a guy would manscape in the Middle Ages." Even so, I look mostly natural again.

When they told me not to shave my body hair, they also gave me the option of wearing a prosthetic cock and balls. That's this rubber device that fits over your whole crotch, with fake pubic hair and everything. They even said I could decide how big I wanted my cock to be. But that seemed stupid. If it looked realistic, everyone would think it was mine anyway. But it probably wouldn't look realistic because prosthetic penises never do, and that would take viewers right out of the movie.

Besides, my real dick looks okay. I'm cut with a decent mushroom head. My cock isn't massive, but I'm a shower not a grower. It wasn't until I started sleeping with guys—and I still haven't had sex with that many guys—that I realized how small some guys' cocks get when they're soft.

Still staring into the mirror, I turn to one side. My stomach is flatter than I realized. And my ass isn't bad either. It's reasonably round with dimples on both sides. It would probably look good filling out a Speedo if I ever dared to wear one.

My eyes return to my cock. It looks pretty good from the side too. Big but pert. No one except a few guys know that I'm a shower not a grower, so anyone looking at me now might think it's massive when I'm hard. It's also proportional, both soft and hard. I guess the term is aesthetically pleasing. That's the other thing I've noticed about seeing other guys' dicks up close and personal: they're not all equally pretty. Some guys' balls hang weird, or their cocks kind of droop, and then there's the whole issue of foreskin. And don't get me started on boners. Those things go all over the place.

No matter what a guy's privates looks like, it's not a deal-breaker for me, not even the size. It would be really ironic for me to reject a guy because of something like that. If I really like a guy, I quickly find myself turned on by the particular look and shape of him, even if I might not have been especially drawn to it before. Because I'm turned on by the person attached to it. That's what happened with Russel, although I have a hard time remembering what it looked like after all these years.

For the first time in my life, looking at my own cock, I realize I have a pretty good one. As in, one that most people would agree is attractive. And I have a pretty good body too. Again, aesthetically pleasing, at least in most people's eyes.

Only a few people have ever seen my body like this. My face might be half freakish, but most of me isn't. My body isn't. Russel told me how handsome he thought I was back at summer camp. And Greg tells me that now.

Now everyone is going to see it.

Here's the funny thing. By having to do this nude scene, and by standing naked in front of this mirror in my trailer, it's like I can finally see it too. For the first time in my life, I can see that I'm actually kind of hot. I won't be thirst-trapping on social media any time soon, but with lighting and makeup, I definitely look better than average. Before, when Russel and Greg said stuff like that, I always nodded and thanked them for the compliments, but I never believed them. I thought they were saying it out of pity. To be nice. It never occurred to me that anyone could ever truly see beyond my scars.

But now I see that even my scars aren't that horrifying. They're even kind of interesting, like a new kind of tattoo. I'm unique, I'll tell you that.

So I guess that's why I'm not very nervous. Because what I'm feeling right now is mirroring exactly what my character is experiencing in the story. And it's nice to be feeling these positive emotions, and exciting to get to be the actor who communicates all this cool stuff to the world.

I'm also happy because I realize what I'm feeling right now is exactly what Russel wanted for me all along.

Forty minutes later, I'm standing out on location, next to a little brook wearing nothing but my robe and some flip-flops. In front of me is a beautiful stretch of trees and grass and flowers. It smells like spring, sweet and fresh. I really could be back in the Middle Ages, as long as I don't turn around.

But then I do turn around, and I'm confronted by this massive tangle of modern equipment: cameras and lights and cords and monitors, everything safely under plastic tarps in case it rains. There are also heating lamps just out of the shot because, well, it's not exactly warm, and I'm about to be completely naked. There's no dialogue until the very end of this scene, which is a good thing since there's no place to hide even the smallest of body-mics on me. They'll use the boom to record the ambient noise, but they might not use any of it because of the heaters, assuming they leave them on. They can add all the sound later anyway, even my breathing.

The fact that they called me from the trailer means they're ready for me to start rehearsals, so I kick off my flip-flops and start to slip off my robe.

"You don't need to..." the lone hair-and-makeup woman starts to say. She's telling me that I don't need to take off my robe for the rehearsal.

But I nod like I know what I'm doing. I hand her the robe. "I want to. I want to get used to being naked in front of everyone, so when we're rolling, I can concentrate on the character."

She smiles like she's impressed with me. Then, as she's turning away with my robe and flip-flops, she sneaks a quick peek at my crotch.

I don't care. If I were her, I'd probably have done the same thing. But I know I have to deal with this somehow.

So, fully naked, I turn and face the crew under the plastic tarps. It's essential crew only, so there are about twenty people—about half as many as usual.

"Can I have everyone's attention?" I say.

People look my way, but no one looks directly at me, because, well, I'm naked.

I lift my arms and thrust my pelvis out, giving everyone a clear view of everything there is to see. "So I'm naked, and everyone knows I'm naked. And I think it'll be easier for me if everyone takes a good long look now and gets it out of the way. Okay?"

Silence falls over the set. And no one looks at my dick. If anything, people seem more uncomfortable.

"I mean it," I say, pointing down to my dick. "You can look. I mean, only if you want to. I'm not trying to sexually harass anyone." Part of me can't believe I'm doing this, but another part of me knows it's the right thing to do.

When I mention sexual harassment, everyone laughs. And people actually do look, even the three other women. The point is to lighten the mood, to eliminate the tension on everyone's part, and it's working. I encourage them with a little naked bump and grind. Everyone laughs louder. I even get a catcall or two.

I have officially won the crowd, which is pretty damn impressive considering that it's mostly a group of dumpy, middle-aged technicians.

From within the crowd, I see Russel grinning, his eyes sparkling. I'm pulling this off even better than he expected.

Finally, Gabriel and Aaron return from over where they'd been consulting with the script supervisor, and people settle down. Director on the set!

"Shall we rehearse?" Gabriel says to everyone, but mostly to me. He seems surprised that I'm already na-ked, and looks everywhere except at my crotch, ner-vous, which makes me wish I'd done my bump and grind thing after he'd joined us. But I do notice that Aaron takes a good long look whether he heard me asking or not. Weirdly, this makes me blush.

At the same time, out of the corner of my eye, I see Russel again, and he's peeking at my dick too. No, at my whole body. He's trying to hide it, but I can tell. He hasn't seen me naked in more than ten years, and he seems to like what he sees. This makes me smile to my-self, because as much as Russel is trying to give my character a clear arc, and also make people see Otto Digmore the actor as a sort of sex object, I don't think *he's* seen me as a true sex object for a long, long time. So I like that I'm surprising him.

We've already rehearsed all the blocking for this scene back in Los Angeles. But I didn't know what the actual set would be like, even though they showed me photographs, so now we go through the whole thing here on location.

At the start of the scene, I'm naked, crouching in the stream, washing myself, but facing away from the camera. Then, finished, I stand, shaking the water off me, and step up onto the grass. Finally, I turn toward the sun, so my body will dry a bit before I get dressed again. I even close my eyes. At this point, the camera will only see me from the waist up.

Then Mika steps out of some trees. She's also coming to bathe.

She sees me, and stops suddenly. But she doesn't leave. She watches me, but my eyes are closed, so I still don't know she's there.

Now the camera sees my whole body, exactly the way Mika does. She—and the whole world—has a clear shot of the goods.

I sense her standing there, and I open my eyes. I gasp and hurry to cover myself. I'm embarrassed and confused because I don't understand the expression on her face.

She's smiling.

But why?

Then I wonder: did she like what she saw? But how could Mika, the confident and beautiful Chinese contortionist, possibly be attracted to me, a disfigured street rat thief?

Finally, I smile back. And we share a moment of connection, both of us desperately wanting something from the other, and realizing we might really get it.

Then Felicia calls to me from nearby, and I pull on my clothes and go to join her, and the moment between Mika and me is over. At least for now.

We do a couple of rehearsals of the whole scene, start to finish. I am expecting the water to be cold, because, come on, it's England in May, but it's even colder than I expect. When I look down at myself, I see that it hasn't had any impact on my dick, but it has made my balls tighter. But that's okay, because it ends up making my dick look bigger.

We do the first couple shots, which I think go great. By this point, I'm feeling nothing but pure excitement, not any nervousness at all. I'm in the zone, and in the moment too. I can't see how this scene could go any better than it already is.

Then it comes time to reposition the camera for the next part of the scene, and I slip my robe back on, because I know it will be a while. Gabriel confers with Aaron and some of his crew, including the director of photography.

Once again, I overhear him.

"We can all see his dick," Gabriel says. "There's no reason why the rest of the world has to see it too."

And Aaron nods like this is the smartest thing he's ever heard.

I'm confused. From the angle of the camera now, it almost looks like it won't see me naked at all, at least not from the front. Did they swap the order of the shots without telling me?

Russel steps up next to Gabriel, and now they talk, but too quietly for me to hear over the babble of the brook and the thrum of the heaters. But I can tell from his body language that Russel is upset. He's as stiff as a scarecrow.

The hair-and-makeup woman hands me a cup of a coffee. This really does feel like it might take a while. Then again, I still have no idea what they're talking about.

Russel's voice rises above the noise. "But the whole point is how *vulnerable* he is. And we need to see what Mika sees, to make their reactions make sense."

I'm instantly tense, because no one's supposed to question the director on the set of a movie, especially the screenwriter. I hope Russel knows what he's doing. But I'm also worried because it sounds like Gabriel is rethinking this entire scene. Or at least shooting it in a way that makes it different from what I thought it was.

The two of them keep talking, and I drift over toward Allison, scarfing Chex Mix at the crafts table. She isn't in makeup and costume because she doesn't appear in the scene, but she showed up anyway, to call to us from off-camera at the end.

"What's going on?" I ask her. No one tells actors anything, so we do our best to eavesdrop and share what we know.

"It sounds like Gabriel's a no-go on the nudity," she says. "Which figures. Straight directors try to get every female on screen topless, but show them a little peen and their heads explode."

"But..." This is what I was afraid she'd say. I was nervous about the scene when Russel first told me, but now I'm all in. And the idea that I might not get to be naked for the whole world to see is suddenly incredibly disappointing. I was even getting used to the idea of being a sort of sex symbol. Not only that, Russel is right: the whole point of the scene is to show Dodge's vulnerability, to show a piece of his character arc. It's stuff like this that will make the scene we shot the day before make sense—the ending when everyone is happy, not because we stole the treasure, but because we're all together and accepted. If they shoot me from the waist up, we won't see what Mika sees, and her reaction won't make any sense. In the end, her and Dodge's relationship won't have nearly the same impact.

I think, Why didn't this come up during rehearsals? I guess because we talked motivation and performance back in Los Angeles, not camera angles.

Gabriel and Russel keep conferring, and it seems tense, but not that tense, mostly because I can tell Russel is holding back. Trying to be agreeable.

They break up at last, and I'm really curious what's going to happen next. Gabriel is still talking with his team, and Aaron is nodding like one of those drinking bird toys. I figure I have a few minutes before the shoot begins again.

I make eye contact with Russel, and I jerk my head, motioning him away from the set.

We drift away, both looking completely casual, aimless, not at all like the screenwriter and actor are teaming up against their director.

We meet in a little copse of trees.

"What was that all about?" I ask.

Russel rubs his face. "It's no big deal. Nothing you need to worry about."

"Russel? Tell me what's going on."

He won't look me in the eye. "He's…making some changes."

"He doesn't think I look good enough, does he? I knew I should have worked out more."

Russel's eyes bore into mine like a drill. "No! I'm *glad* you didn't work out more. It's perfect for the scene exactly the way it is. *You're* perfect."

"What kind of changes?"

He softens his expression. "Otto, don't worry about it. Everything's going to be fine. The director of photography sided with me, so I got Gabriel to agree to shoot it both ways—his way and mine. I mean, with the nudity and without. And once they get to editing, I'm absolutely positive he'll see I'm right about the scene."

As usual, Russel isn't a good enough actor to make me think he believes what he's saying. The truth is, he's freaked out because Gabriel is turning out to be a disappointing director.

Allison had suggested that we actors try power-bottoming our way to decent performances, but that's harder than I thought. And now I see there's a lot more to a movie than good acting anyway. Camera angles, for one thing—and everything else the director does. The actors can all give great performances, but Gabriel can still screw the whole thing up.

Russel will be crushed. I can't let that happen, not after everything he's done for me.

But what can I do? I'm just an actor. Today, I'm not even wearing any clothes.

CHAPTER NINE

Five days later, the production is supposed to have its first day off. I had planned to ask Russel if he wanted to go into Nottingham with me, but the day before, I realize I'm pretty tired from all the excitement of the shoot, and I decide to spend the day ordering room service and marathoning *The Chilling Adventures of Sabrina* alone in my room. It's a surprisingly good show, especially since *Riverdale* is so bad.

I also finally have a long Facetime chat with Greg—to fill him in on everything that's gone on. Except I find myself blunting the truth a bit. I mean, things have gone okay since the day of my maybe-or-maybe-not nude scene. But most of the stuff we've shot since then has been really easy. The different characters riding through the forest on horseback or walking in and out of Shirell Castle. They would be hard for any director to screw up.

Late in the afternoon, Russel texts me to ask if I want to go to dinner, and I say okay, suggesting the restaurant in Thoresby Hall. But I'm not entirely sure I want to be alone with him. I've seen him almost every day on the set, and we've been alone together there, but not alone-alone. Not alone where we can talk openly about Gabriel. Part of me doesn't want to depress him about how the movie's going. Or maybe I don't want him depressing me.

I send my driver to pick him up, and we agree to meet in the Great Hall, which is what they call the lobby. The entire hotel is really nice. It's obvious that whatever dukes lived here before they turned it into a hotel were fantastically rich. I can't help but think it's kind of wasted on me and the other actors, who have been spending twelve to fourteen hours a day on the set, but I'm kind of a movie star now, and I'm not going to turn it down when someone offers to put me up in a place like this.

I see Russel before he sees me, and he's looking around, impressed by the plush furniture, and the iron-wrought chandeliers hanging overhead. The walls are dotted with the mounted heads of stags, which is a little creepy but also the kind of thing a place like this should have.

"The bedrooms are drafty, and the bathroom pipes squeak," I say, coming up behind him.

"Really?" Russel says, brightening hopefully.

"No, but the first night I was here, I didn't realize they'd left a chocolate on my pillow, and I slept on it, and it melted out of the foil, and now I'm worried the maid thinks I shit the bed."

Russel laughs out loud, and I smile. I really like making him laugh.

We work our way to the restaurant, which is also really nice—a massive parlor with more high ceilings, and this intricate blue wallpaper, and a grand fireplace filled with what is either a real fire or the most convincing fake one I've ever seen. The booths are half-circles, covered with plush light blue velvet, obviously custom made. We haven't even sat down, and I'm already worried I'm going to spill.

We pass Clayton Beck and his entourage at one of the tables, and I secretly hope he'll notice us and invite us to join him for dinner. Maybe get the waiters to pull another table up against theirs, although I'm not sure they do stuff like that in a place like this. It's partly because I'm still not sure I want to be alone with Russel, because of the whole Gabriel thing. But mostly I just want to have dinner with Clayton Beck. I'm now up to seventeen sentences that I've spoken to him, but a lot of those have been things like, "Hi, how are you doing?"

He doesn't notice us.

"By the way," Russel says as we settle into our booth, "you don't need to pay for my dinner."

Then he opens his menu and sees the prices, and his eyes shoot open in alarm.

"No," I say. "I invited you, so I've got this. Well, the studio does."

Russel lowers his menu. "The studio?"

I can't help blushing. "Um, the studio gave me a credit card for…you know. Stuff like this."

"They gave you a *credit card*? I asked my agent if they'd pay for *my* meals, and he told me to save all my receipts, but not to get my hopes up."

I'm about to tell Russel that the credit card does have a three hundred dollar daily limit, but then I realize that will sound even worse. It really is shocking the different way Hollywood treats leading actors and screenwriters. But this might be the only studio movie I ever do, and I'm still not about to turn down free money.

"In *that* case," Russel says, glaring defiantly at the menu, "I'm ordering the most expensive thing on the menu, which is…" His face falls. "Rump of lamb with black pudding and jellied eel." He hesitates a second, and then says with perfect comic timing, "Okay, so maybe I'm having the *second* most expensive item on the menu. The grilled lobster." He slams his menu closed with a dramatic flourish.

Now I laugh. Russel makes me laugh a lot too.

I study the menu, even though I already know what I want: a ribeye steak with baked garlic mushrooms. I'm still not ready to hear what Russel thinks about Gabriel.

Finally, the waiter comes to bring our drinks, and also take our order. When we're done, he also takes my menu, which means I can't hide behind it anymore.

"So," I say.

"So," Russel says, and part of me wonders if he's nervous about talking to me too.

"How's your guesthouse anyway?" I'm not looking to emphasize the difference between his lodging and mine again, but it's better than talking about the movie.

"It's okay. The owner seems a little judge-y, so I find myself cleaning up every morning before I leave, which sucks. We're paying her, right? I mean, the studio's probably not paying very *much*, but they've got to be paying something."

I laugh, but it doesn't feel quite as genuine this time.

Allison and Ying pass by, following the hostess to a table of their own. But unlike Clayton Beck, they notice us right away.

"Otto!" Allison says, her face lighting up. "And the world's best best friend, Russel Middlebrook."

After we all greet each other, Russel and I exchange a glance, the same question on both our faces: Should we ask them to eat with us?

Finally, Russel says, "You guys wanna join us?"

"You sure?" Ying says. "We don't want to intrude."

"No, it's okay," Russel and I say at exactly the same time. Then we laugh almost entirely in sync too. It's awkward because it's obvious something is going on. I didn't want to be alone with Russel, but I'm not crazy about realizing he didn't want to be alone with me either.

Ying hesitates, but Allison slides right into our booth. Then Ying tentatively pulls up a chair.

"So," Russel says, "I have a confession to make."

"Oh?" Allison says, perking up. "Do tell."

"Most people didn't actually ride horses in the Middle Ages, at least in England. Except for the very wealthy, most people didn't go anywhere. They spent their whole lives in the town or city where they were born. I mean, a blacksmith probably wouldn't own a horse, and might not even know how to ride one. A really successful male architect might, but not his daughter."

"Then why...?" I start to say.

"Because everyone always rides horses in the movies set in the Middle Ages. So now people think they were like cars, and it's how everyone got around. Plus, it really helped with the plot, especially the end. I mean, there was no way they were getting away without horses, not carrying all that treasure."

I can't help but smile. It's true that Russel is cutting some historical corners, which I suppose is bad, but at least he's aware of it, and he's got good reasons. And once again, he's reminding me how movies both mirror reality and also help shape it.

"Your secret is safe with us," I say at last, taking a drink of my beer.

"So," Allison says, "how much of an idiot is Gabriel?"

It's all I can do not to spit out my beer. So much for avoiding the topic of how the movie is going. I should have expected this the second Allison sat down.

She looks at me, confused by my reaction. "What?"

"Nothing," I choke out. "I was trying to avoid talking about that."

"You were?" Russel says. "So was I!"

We all have a good laugh, and Ying says, "Gabriel's bad, but I've had worse directors."

"Really?" I say. Ying probably has more credits than any of us, even if they're mostly small, supporting roles, so I'm eager to hear what she has to say.

She thinks for a second, and then says, "Well, maybe not on a studio film."

So much for my being excited.

"He hasn't done anything *that* bad," Russel says. "He did agree to shoot Otto's nude scene both ways."

So Russel is trying to be optimistic like me.

Then Allison waggles an eyebrow, and leans into me. "Otto's *nude* scene."

I can't help but blush at her teasing, and I'm glad when Ying changes the subject. "But in a couple of weeks, we start shooting the interiors. Then shit gets real."

Allison fake-coughs and mutters, "Power bottom," then fake-coughs again.

"What's that?" Russel says.

"Nothing," I say, giving Allison the fish eye. I definitely don't want to discuss Allison's theory of the director-actor relationship in front of Russel, so I quickly change the subject. "Are we even absolutely sure Gabriel's screwing things up? I mean, how many stories have you guys heard about movie sets where the movie was supposed to be a disaster, but it turned out great? Wasn't the *Casablanca* set a complete mess?"

Russel nods along. "And *The African Queen*. And *Jaws*. And *The Wizard of Oz*. And *Apocalypse Now*. And *Star Wars*. Yeah, lots of great movies."

"So maybe there's hope," I say, forcing out a smile.

"You really think Gabriel is making *The Wizard of Oz*?" Allison says, motioning to the waiter like she's desperate to have him come and take her drink order.

I nod, conceding her point.

Ying is suddenly thoughtful. "It *is* true that you usually have no idea if a movie's going to be any good from the shoot. I've been in terrible movies that felt on the set like they were going to be awesome."

"And when things seem bad on the set, the movie turns out great?" I ask.

"No, those movies turn out terrible too."

Allison snorts.

"Well, what's the set like when the movie turns out really good?" I ask Ying.

She looks glum. "I wouldn't know—I've never been in a really good movie."

We laugh hard, and I almost spit my beer again. People in Hollywood talk like this a lot, like they know how many shitty studio movies the industry churns out, especially compared to television, which is so obviously better and smarter than most of what you see in theaters.

"I'm not sure Gabriel has any idea what my screenplay is about," Russel says, as glum as Ying.

"It's not fair," I say. "After all the shit you and I have been through?" I acknowledge Allison and Ying. "What *all of us* have been through. We finally get a chance to show what we can do, and Gabriel is going to screw it all up?"

Everyone agrees it's not fair, but Allison and Ying don't look quite as put out as Russel and me, either because they've already had more success than we have, or because they're women and used to shit like this.

Right then, the waiter comes to take Allison and Ying's orders. As they're talking, I make a decision.

Once the waiter's gone, I say to the table, "We need to do something."

Everyone stares at me.

"About Gabriel," I go on. Before Allison can bring up her theory about power bottoming your way to good performance again, I add, "Not just about our individual performances. We need to do something to make sure Gabriel doesn't ruin the movie."

Allison laughs like I'm making a joke. A second later, Ying joins in, but Russel doesn't.

"I'm *serious*," I say.

Ying stops laughing. "He's the director," she says, sounding mystified. "There's nothing we can do. Is there?" In a way, she's right. The director of a movie is like the captain of a ship: whatever they say goes. But unlike a ship, when a movie sinks, it's the entire cast that goes down with it, not just the director.

I look directly at Russel. "Come on. You must have some idea."

"*Me?* I'm just the screenwriter. The guy who's staying in the guesthouse with cockroaches, not Thoresby fucking *Hall.*"

Allison and Ying laugh, and this time I smile.

"Five months ago, you told me you were done playing by someone else's rules," I say. "That you were going to do whatever it took to get ahead in Hollywood."

Allison tilts her head, suddenly very intrigued. She and Ying look from me, then back to Russel again, waiting for his answer.

"Yeah," he says, nodding along, "but that was before I finally had a studio movie go into production. Besides, it was also complete bullshit. I mean, what does that even *mean*, playing by your own rules? Anyway, you're the big movie star with the big fat studio credit card. What are *you* going to do about it?"

I open my mouth like I have some kind of answer, but nothing comes out. Because there really isn't an answer, at least not one that I can see. On a movie set, the director is king.

Right then, the salads arrive, and when the waiter leaves, I change the topic again, so I don't have to admit I don't have any answers either.

Russel and I never do make it to Nottingham, even though it's only twenty kilometers away. And before we know it, everyone is getting ready to leave Sherwood Forest for Malta, this island-country in the Mediterranean, which is where the rest of the movie will be shot. Supposedly, it has this great movie studio where they film a lot of fantasy-type movies or TV shows, including *Game of Thrones*. It also has a lot of ancient castles.

In Malta, we'll mostly be shooting interiors, which is where shit does get real, like Ying said. This is where the important stuff happens: the characters planning the heist, and then pulling it off. That's the whole second half of the movie.

One of the interesting things about Russel's screenplay is that the challenges the characters face aren't the usual challenges for a movie like this. In a castle in the Middle Ages, there weren't any security cameras or alarm systems that had to be deactivated, or fingerprint or retina scans that needed to be outwitted, and the castle guards didn't have phones or walkie-talkies or any other way to communicate with each other. Also, any treasure wasn't locked behind some impenetrable vault, because things like that didn't exist yet. It was behind regular doors.

But that doesn't mean it's easy for us thieves. If anything, it's harder. Rather than alarm systems, the castle uses actual human guards, who are everywhere, all heavily armed, with instructions to swing first and ask questions later. Also, while there's no technology in the castle, we thieves don't have any technology either, which means we have no way to contact each other if something goes wrong, and also no way to bypass locked doors except with old-fashioned ingenuity. We're also stealing gold, which is really heavy. And we have to get it out beyond the stone walls, then far away from the castle, without anyone knowing.

Here's how Russel spells out the actual heist part of the movie in the script.

Benjamin Smith suggests we try scaling the castle walls at night. But using a model of the castle, Felicia argues that the whole point of the walls is to keep invaders out, even one single invader who could unlock the front gate and let an army inside. She explains about the moat, and the sheer walls, and the guards with torches who are constantly walking back and forth, looking down from the ramparts. She points out that there are latrines sticking out from some of the walls, but that the hole for the toilet isn't big enough to climb up through.

So she finally convinces us that the only option is to enter the castle walls during the day, when the gates are wide open, pretending to seek an audience with the king. Later, after some group planning, Benjamin describes how the plan is supposed to go.

First, we'll be searched for weapons at the front gate, so I'll hide my thieving tools in plain sight, stitched into an adornment on the front of my jersey. Once we make it inside the castle, we somehow have to get from the throne room to the treasure room, which is in a completely different part of the castle. So while in the throne room, Gordo will use sleight of hand and his bag of tricks to create a distraction. At that, the rest of us can duck into a side hallway that leads to a secret passageway—an escape passage for the king in case of an invasion.

This gets us close to the treasure room where we'll knock the guards out with a smoke bomb made of opium, henbane, mulberry juice, hemlock, mandragora, and ivy. It's so specific that I figure Russel must be describing something real.

Once the guards are asleep, Benjamin, Felicia, Mika, and I will breathe from large bison bladders full of air. As the thief, I'll unlock the door using my secret tools. Then it's simply a question of carting the gold to the closest latrine, where we will drop the gold down into the moat. Since this latrine is facing away from the road into the castle, no one will see, and then we come back to retrieve the gold the following night, after everything settles down.

At this point, the script swings to real life: the five of us pulling off the heist. But this being a movie, nothing goes according to plan. For example, my thieving tools are too *much* in plain sight, and the guards confiscate them because they look suspicious.

And Gordo's diversion makes the guards more suspicious, and it turns out the secret passage we need never got built. At each point, we have to improvise. We dress up like guards. When we finally get to the treasure room, the smoke bombs don't work, so we have to knock out the guards by hand. I use straw from a broom and a piece of cutlery to pick the lock on the treasure room door.

Finally, we do get the gold, which we load on to our cloaks, flat on the floor. Then we slide it down the hallway, toward the nearest latrine.

At the same time, King Gilbert and the guards arrive at the treasure room, and see that gold has been taken. But the captain of the guard immediately says, "The latrine! Whoever did this, they're going to drop the gold down into the moat."

This is where the script pulls off a bit of mis-direction. Benjamin, Felicia, and Dodge, hiding nearby, all heave a sigh of relief because we've since changed the plan. We're *not* on our way to the latrine. Instead, we take the gold to a nearby window where Mika has been using her acrobatic skills to create a clever leverage system that will lower the gold down to Gordo, waiting with a cart in an alley below.

From there, we head for the front gates of the castle, having put on new costumes back in the alley: we're now a priest and a family of mourners, pulling a cart with a coffin on it. The guards are on very high alert, but we don't look like thieves, because Gordo is now pretending to be a frail old man, and Mika is so small she could only be a child, and, well, I'm a scarred freak who brings people bad luck. Even better, we've put the rotting head of a dead moose inside the coffin. Because it stinks so bad, they assume it must really be a dead body, and the guards don't bother looking inside.

Outside the gates, we cross paths with the king himself, who's increasingly desperate, overseeing the search for the gold somewhere in the moat. But he doesn't pay us any attention, and even ends up getting shit on by someone using a latrine up in the castle. Meanwhile, we head for the safety of the nearby woods—which will eventually lead to the very first scene we shot, the last one in the movie, where everyone says goodbye, but ends up deciding to travel on together anyway.

Like everything in Russel's script, it's all pretty clever and also historically plausible. I didn't know that Europe had both bison and moose in the eleventh century, but according to Russel, they did.

About half the scenes will be filmed on soundstages. The other half will take place inside different ancient castles and buildings all around the island, and also on the northern Maltese island of Gozo.

We'll be filming in Malta for seven weeks. But I'll know long before then if *Blackburn Castle* is going to be a disaster.

I'll also know if this movie is going to destroy what's left of Russel's and my careers.

CHAPTER TEN

Malta isn't what I expect.

I read up on it on the plane. Because it's located right in the middle of the Mediterranean—a strategic location for all the countries who used to want to conquer the Known World—people have been fighting over it for thousands of years.

But once we land, and Russel and I grab our luggage and meet my driver, I see that Malta is shockingly dry. More like Africa than Europe. You can count the number of trees on one hand. And all the buildings are really old, made of this yellowish limestone. That looks like Africa too, or maybe the Middle East.

I turn to Russel. "*Blackburn Castle* is set in England, right?"

He nods. "In 1142 AD."

"But Malta doesn't look like England. Are the castles the same?"

"Well, that's the thing. There are differences, but the climate here is a lot drier, so the castles are much better preserved. So they had to decide: do they go for the more accurate-looking castle interiors, or the better-preserved ones? It's harder to fix interiors with CGI."

He clears his throat and gives me a wry little smile. "So you see? It's not just me who's fudging facts here and there."

I smile too and look back out the window.

My hotel is closer, and my driver stops there first. I'm worried that Russel will see that it's another grand luxury place, and then he'll find out he's in some cheap bed and breakfast. And yeah, it does look like a pretty nice place from the outside, like it was once a castle itself.

"I'll text you later and we can go to dinner, okay?" I say.

"Sure," he says even as I'm closing the door in his face.

The inside of the hotel is even more impressive than the outside. The lobby has these tall arched stone ceilings, and a fountain that runs down one entire wall. After I check in, I see my room has this incredibly cool sink and bathtub that look like they were carved right out of the limestone, like they're just part of the building.

I don't want Russel to see, so I make a point to meet him at the restaurant tonight for dinner, not back here. I just hope I can keep him away from my hotel for the entire rest of the shoot.

The next day, Gabriel invites all the key players from the movie out to dinner in Valletta, which is the one big city on Malta. My driver takes Russel and me as close as he can to the restaurant, but it's located down a narrow stone street that's only accessible by foot.

It's a nice Italian restaurant, and the hostess leads us to a big private room in the back, with one really long table that seats at least forty people. Russel and I greet everyone: Allison and Ying, and yes, Gabriel and Aaron. We act like it's been forever since we've seen each other, even hugging, which is kind of silly, because we were together in England only two days ago. But this is an entirely different country, so it feels like a fresh start.

I also try to talk to Clayton Beck, but every time I do, one of the members of his entourage steps in front of me, blocking him, and I'm now certain they do that kind of thing on purpose. I'm up to twenty-nine sentences that I've spoken to him, but I still don't have a single good anecdote to share on any talk shows.

Finally, we all sit. There aren't assigned seats or anything, at least I don't think there are, but somehow Gabriel ends up at the head of the table, with Clayton Beck, his leading man, sitting at his right, and Allison, the leading lady, sitting on his left. I remember reading something about how medieval kings arranged the people at their tables in order of their importance to the crown, and I can't help but wonder if Gabriel had done this too—informally, I mean. Or maybe it's Allison and Clayton being smart enough to suck up to him. Who knew Clayton Beck was a power bottom too?

Despite our best efforts, Russel and I end up in seats much farther down the table, past Ying, and even farther than Victor Bowers. Aaron takes a seat near us, which is kind of flattering because it feels like maybe he's trying to spy on us.

Right after we order our drinks, Gabriel clicks his water glass with a fork. We all quiet down, and he says,

"I just want to tell everyone that I've got some really good news. So far, the studio really likes the dailies!"

The dailies are the raw, unedited footage from the different days' shooting. According to everything I've ever heard, it's really hard to predict whether a movie will be any good based on the dailies. Along with no editing, there's no music or sound effects, or color-correcting, and the audio is bad. Still, if the dailies are downright awful, that does mean something.

For a moment, no one says anything. We all look around the table at each other, but no one quite reacts, except for Aaron, who is nodding and smiling like this news is totally expected, like nothing weird or stupid has happened so far on set or in rehearsal. He's such a perfect little suck-up.

The rest of us, the people who aren't suck-ups, are trying to make sense of what Gabriel's told us. Is it possible the studio really does like what Gabriel is doing? Maybe it's an ironic thing, like, Oh, of *course* the studio would like mediocre work. Or maybe the studio somehow expected him to screw it up, but he hasn't yet, so they're pleasantly surprised.

Finally, Clayton Beck says, "That's great, Gabriel. Really, really great."

This breaks the logjam, and everyone else also congratulates him. We all congratulate each other too, kind of.

"There's even talk about a springtime release," Gabriel goes on.

If this is true, this is also good news, potentially, because the studios always release the movies they think will make the most money in the spring or early summer. But part of me doesn't believe this either, because spring is when the studios release their blockbusters, and we're not really that kind of movie. We're a late summer release. A bit more humble and modest.

I look over at Russel, who looks exactly like I feel: skeptical, but trying hard to be hopeful. I think back on what Russel said about how chaotic movie sets often lead to great, even classic movies. Why couldn't that still be us?

Gabriel laughs. "All I can say is, 'Really?' Because I was starting to think I was fucking the whole thing up!"

The whole table immediately bursts into laughter, because—let's face it—this is the first truly smart thing most of us have ever heard Gabriel say. And people keep laughing even after Aaron and Gabriel stop, and I'm secretly hoping they both understand what this means. That it's kind of a sick burn.

Two waiters enter, carrying these four massive plates of antipasto, and everyone finally settles down again. After delivering the food, the waiters go along the table to get everyone's order. But this takes a long time, and we're way down at the end, so we talk amongst ourselves.

Russel leans into me. "What do you think? Is he telling the truth about the studio liking the dailies?"

"He might be," I say. "I don't think he knows enough about acting to tell that good a lie."

At that, Russel laughs, and I laugh too, and Aaron looks over at us, and I get nervous and freeze up, because it feels like he knows what we're laughing about.

Even so, I'm definitely feeling hopeful again—or at least a little less skeptical. The studio likes the dailies? They're considering a prime release date?

I dish up some antipasto, and the salami is really good, but the pepper is ridiculously hot.

After the waiters have finally taken everyone's order and left, Gabriel pipes up again. "I don't want this whole dinner to be us talking shop, but as you all know, we're about to start shooting the interiors, which is the real heart of this film. Actors, this is the most important character work you'll be doing on this movie, and it's also the stuff that's most important to the plot. Basically, if we're going to screw up this movie, this is where we're going to do it."

Russel and I both nod, and I realize that almost everyone else is nodding too—a little too emphatically, which is kind of another sick burn. Still, what he said just now about this being the heart of the film is exactly right, and we're all totally with him.

"I think it's ironic we're doing this movie right now," Gabriel goes on, "and at the same time back home in America, the whole country is having this big debate about whether we should build a big wall along our southern border. Because that's what this movie is about too: walls. Who builds them and what they mean. The physical walls that divide the rich from the poor, but also the psychological walls between people. The ones each of us build to keep other people out."

Beside me, I see Russel blinking hard, like he's been blinded by a great light and is now very confused. I'm confused too. All that stuff about walls? It's almost like Gabriel overheard Russel talking at that first read-through. But he hadn't been nearby. So were we wrong about Gabriel? Does he somehow truly understand Russel's script?

All of a sudden, I feel lighter than air, like my head might bump up against the ceiling, like it's an escaped helium balloon. If Gabriel really does understand the script, maybe the movie won't suck, and I really am going to be able to show the world what I can do. Maybe things are not at all what they seemed, and it finally is going to happen for me. And Russel.

I sense a new energy in the seats around me, like everyone else is lighter than air too, like we're all a bunch of helium balloons, loose and carefree. They're all reacting to Gabriel's speech like I am.

I realize how ravenous I am, and I dish up more antipasto. I'm not the only one. A lot of people are realizing they're hungry.

The cheeses are even better than the cured meat. This seems like a really good restaurant—the first of many great restaurants I'll be eating in, every day for the rest of my life.

"But I am a little concerned about the tone," Gabriel goes on. "Everything is coming across pretty grim. So I'm hoping the next seven weeks give us a chance to find the humor in this story."

I'm a little surprised by this observation. There are a few jokes in *Blackburn Castle*, and they're pretty funny. But they're character-based. This isn't a movie with a funny tone. It's a story that takes itself very seriously, because it's a very serious story for the characters. For them, this heist is the most important thing they've ever done. If they fail, they'll all be executed. But if they succeed, they'll get everything they ever wanted, and the treasure is the absolute least of it.

So I'm suddenly back to being confused. It feels like the rest of the table is too. I happen to be biting down on a piece of the same salami that was so good before, but now I can barely taste it in my mouth.

Gabriel keeps talking, like he's sharing a secret with us. "I know I'm not supposed to say this, because the movie was a big bomb. But the one thing I liked about the *Robin Hood* reboot was the tone. It wasn't afraid to be cheeky. Self-aware. Not too much, of course. But who knows? In the weeks ahead, there might even be an opportunity for us to use those two glorious words, slapstick."

I immediately think: Slapstick is one word, not two. Even I know that, and I'm not a writer.

Sitting next to me, Russel slides deeper into his seat.

Gabriel doesn't understand Russel's script, not at all. The last thing this movie needs is ironic cheekiness, and there's definitely no place anywhere for slapstick. As for those things he said about breaking through walls, maybe he did overhear Russel that day at the read-through. Or, more likely, Aaron did, and he told Gabriel, and he's been using Russel's ideas to impress people ever since.

Everyone stops eating. Chairs squeak. Everyone knows what Russel and I know, which is that Gabriel's ideas couldn't be more wrong.

Except for Aaron, of course, who can barely keep from applauding. "I love it!" he gushes.

I start in on the antipasto again, because I don't know what else to do, and I even bite down on another one of those really hot peppers, but this time I swallow it down, no problem at all, and I'm barely even aware of the heat.

From that point on, the atmosphere in the room is strange.

On the surface, everyone is happy. It's a dinner party! We're in Malta! We're filming a *movie*!

But I'm an actor: I know subtext when I see it. Gabriel has dropped a serious turd in the punchbowl, and now no one dares to fish it out. Instead, we all go on drinking the punch, and we know we're going to have to keep drinking that punch for the next seven weeks.

Gabriel doesn't seem to notice. Maybe he's too clueless. Or maybe he knows he's the director, and it doesn't matter what anyone else thinks.

"What do you think of your hotel?"

It's Aaron, across the table from me.

"Huh?" I say. "Oh. It's nice."

Aaron's lips make a knowing little smile. Gabriel may not have noticed the room's subtext, but Aaron did. And for some reason, he thinks it has to do with me.

"The building of that hotel is four hundred years old," he goes on. "Well, at *least* four hundred years. It's probably a lot older than that, but records only go back that far. It's the nicest hotel on the island."

I nod. "Well, it's definitely nice. My bathtub is carved out of limestone."

Aaron nods, then turns to Russel. He doesn't say anything, but he keeps smiling.

And finally, I understand what Aaron is doing. The whole point was to have me acknowledge I'm staying in a nice hotel so Aaron can subtly rub Russel's face in the fact that he has to stay in some shitty bed and breakfast. He's trying to drive a wedge between Russel and me. Or something.

The guy is annoying as shit, but I have to admit, he ain't stupid.

Russel doesn't take the bait like I knew he wouldn't.

Instead, he says, not to Aaron but to the whole table around us, "Earlier, I was reading about something called the Malta Fungus. Back in the sixteenth century, a local order of knights discovered this 'miracle' plant— it's actually a flowering plant, not a fungus—and it supposedly cured everything from dysentery to venereal disease. But it only grew on top of one rocky little island just offshore of Gozo. Once word got out about this plant, everyone wanted some, even back in Europe, and the knights began charging ridiculously high prices. But poor people had health problems too, and they started taking boats out to the island to harvest it for themselves. The knights became worried that this might drive the plant to extinction, and it also undercut their prices, so they posted guards on the island, declaring that stealing it was punishable by death. They even went so far as to shear off the rocky sides of the island, so people couldn't climb up from some back cove and sneak around in the dark. The only way to reach the top of the island became this primitive cable car from the mainland."

"Does the plant still grow there?" I ask. "And does it really not grow anywhere else in the world?"

Russel looks directly at Aaron for the first time since he started his little story. "It's still there. And it grows in Africa, but that little island is the only place it grows in all of Europe."

"I'll bite," Aaron says. "Is it really a miracle plant like the knights said?"

Russel smiles—the exact same little smirk that Aaron had before, when he asked me about my hotel. "Hardly. It doesn't do any of the things the knights thought it did, and it might even make you sicker. Turns out it was total bullshit."

I have to give it to Russel: he's pretty good at the subtext game. Then again, he's a writer, and subtext is what he does for a living.

Dinner breaks up right after dessert. Russel and I are at the far end of the table, so we're at the back of the crowd as everyone makes their way out of the restaurant, and it takes a while. When we reach the pedestrian street outside, it's way past sunset, and there are no streetlights, so everything is much darker now. It feels like stepping out into a river of shadows.

The rest of the procession moves toward the main road where the drivers are waiting, but Russel and I hold back, lingering by a darkened storefront. Allison and Ying notice, and they fall back too. I'm glad because I want to know what the others think about what Gabriel said during dinner, even though I have a pretty good idea.

Two members of the production team stay behind too. It's David, the DP, and Ethan, the producer I met in Gabriel's office all those months ago. I've since learned that he's the guy who optioned Russel's script in the first place. He's the one who brought it to Disney.

They're both older. David is a big bear of a guy, bald with a big beard and a Santa Claus twinkle in his eye. Ethan is smaller, a little twitchy, with close-cropped wiry hair, and a moustache and soul patch. It's clear they sense what the rest of us are thinking, and they might have something to add.

But none of us says anything, and it's too dark to get a clear read on anyone's expression. We all stand near each other, not quite in a circle. Ethan shuffles his feet.

It's like we're undercover agents meeting for the first time.

"So," Allison says.

"Yeah," David adds.

"Yup," I say.

No one says anything more, and Ying pops a breath mint from a metal tin. Russel is wearing a light jacket, and he pulls it tight, even though it's not at all cold outside. It really is like being undercover agents, because it feels like we're worried the others might sell us out. We don't really know David and Ethan, and they don't know us. So once again, none of us wants to say something bad that might get back to Gabriel.

David lights a cigarette. Allison bums one and lights up too.

Finally, David says, "That was interesting." I know he means the dinner.

"Really interesting," Russel says.

"*Very* interesting," Ethan agrees.

Allison nods and blows a cloud of smoke, off to one side. Even she isn't bold enough to say outright what we're all thinking.

"Gabriel's going to ruin the movie."

In the dark, I'm confused about who spoke. It's a voice with a bit of a drawl—not any of us.

Clayton Beck steps forward out of the shadows, joining our not-quite-a-circle.

Clayton Beck! I never would have guessed that the thirtieth sentence he ever said to me was going to be about what a terrible director Gabriel is. He's without his entourage for once. He must have sent them on ahead in order to have this conversation with us.

Allison blows another cloud of smoke, hard, this time right in all our faces. "Right? *Finally* someone said it. Gabriel *is* going to ruin this movie, because he's a fucking idiot."

"Yes!" David says, holding up his hands like he's finally had his prayers answered.

"He is," I say.

"He's not great," Ying says, crunching down on the breath mint in her mouth.

"Tonight, those were some of the dumbest ideas I've *ever* heard," David says. "And I once worked for Eli Roth."

Russel just sighs, long and low.

I hate seeing Russel like this, and I still don't dare to talk directly to Clayton Beck, so I ask David and Ethan, "Is it just you guys? Or is it the whole production team? Does *everyone* think Gabriel is going to ruin the movie?" The fact is, actors and crew work side-by-side on a movie set, but they don't talk all that much. We tend to stay in our own little groups.

David turns to Ethan, as if to gauge his reaction. "Well, Gabriel's the director," David says, "so no one's going to say anything openly. Especially with Aaron around."

Clayton Beck scoffs. "Aaron."

I elbow Russel, and he snorts. Our first real movie might be going right down the crapper, but at least everyone else hates Aaron as much as we do.

"I *never* wanted Gabriel as the director," Ethan laments. "But the studio insisted, and *Snark* seemed okay, so I hoped for the best. But it's been obvious for a while that his ideas are, uh, shit. And it's only gotten worse since then."

David nods. "Sometimes on a movie set, the director does things you don't understand until later. He has a very specific vision. But you can always tell they *have* a vision. With Gabriel...."

"—there's no vision," Ethan finishes.

Now everyone nods at the same time, slightly out of sync, like cats in a YouTube video. This is like the conversation Russel, Allison, Ying, and I had back in England, except we now know that Gabriel no longer deserves the benefit of the doubt.

"We need to tell the studio," I say. "If they hear the same thing from all of us, they'll have no choice but to replace Gabriel."

Russel perks up. "It'll be like the cabinet of the President and the Twenty-Fifth Amendment!"

Everyone stares at him. I can't see faces clearly, but I somehow know they all have blank, confused expressions.

Russel senses it too. "You know! How the President can be declared incompetent if a majority of his cabinet votes that he is? No, wait, I think they need the vote of the Vice-President too."

No one says anything to this either, and Ethan shuffles his feet again.

"That won't happen," Ethan says at last. "They won't replace him."

"But why—?" Russel starts to say.

"For one thing, I already tried, and they said no. But now we're too far into production. Besides, Gabriel isn't incompetent. He just makes, uh, shitty artistic choices. But that's his right—he's got a contract. He's the director, and it's his job to make the choices. We can't get him fired just because some of us disagree with those choices."

Suddenly, I'm feeling very bold, so I turn to Clayton Beck. "What about you? There must be something *you* can do. You're Clayton Beck."

He sighs. "I tried too. Right after rehearsals started. But it turned out to be harder than I thought."

"Because his dad runs the damn studio," Ethan says. "How do you think he got the job in the first place?"

Clayton nods in the dark, like this is something he already knew.

But I feel a flash of blinding rage. I see now how right Russel was all those months ago—how the rules of Hollywood really do only apply to people like him and me, as a way to shut us out. Meanwhile, the big, important jobs to go to rich, connected people like Gabriel, even if they're totally unqualified. And once they have those jobs, it becomes almost impossible for them to fail.

"We *have* to get rid of Gabriel," I say. "So if we can't get him fired, we have to have him killed."

CHAPTER ELEVEN

I see the whites of everyone's eyes staring back at me in the dark. They're shocked, and I realize that my joke about killing Gabriel didn't sound all that much like a joke.

So I hurry to say, "I'm kidding! You guys really think I'd want to murder Gabriel? Thanks a lot, guys, thanks a lot."

Everyone laughs, and a couple of people snort, and it all echoes against the limestone buildings. Russel laughs louder than anyone. I hope it's because my joke is funny, but I think maybe also he's relieved that I *am* joking.

I laugh along with the others, but I also wonder why my joke didn't sound all that much like a joke. I wouldn't ever really kill Gabriel. But I'm still pissed off about how hard it is for guys like Russel and me to make it in Hollywood when it seems so easy for people like Gabriel.

Then I remember my friend Mo's advice to me, back in Los Angeles, how it's not our experiences in life that define us, but the choices we make after they happen.

This is what she meant. Russel and I finally have our first—and maybe our only—real shot at success. So we need to choose to take advantage of it. We need to do whatever we can—short of murder—to make this movie work.

When the laughter finally dies down, I say, very quietly, "Still …"

This time, no one laughs. Down the street, a rolling metal door slams: a merchant closing up for the night. I catch a foul whiff of an open garbage can somewhere nearby.

"What?" Russel asks me.

"Look, we're all standing here whispering in the dark for a reason," I say. "We all think Gabriel is screwing up the movie and something needs to be done. Right? So whatever we can do—except murder, I mean—let's do it."

No one says anything. Allison exhales more smoke, but she's back to blowing it off to one side.

But Russel isn't convinced. "What can *we* do?"

"Well, for one thing," I say, "we can try talking some sense into him."

David nods approvingly. "Like what you guys have been doing." Everything Russel and I have done so far is probably how he and Ethan—and Clayton Beck— knew we were safe to talk to in the first place.

"And we can stand together," I say. "Support each other when Gabriel has another one of his dumb ideas." Once again, I look directly at Clayton, be- cause—let's face it—other than the director, he's the person with the most power on this movie.

To my relief, his head tips into a nod.

Ethan looks at David, a note of hope in his voice. "We might even be able to, uh...."

David finishes. "Shoot a scene or two behind his back? If we have to, yeah."

"What good would that do?" Ying asks.

"At least the movie won't be locked into Gabriel's stupid choices. It'll preserve our options later on. Like what Russel did with Otto's nude scene."

"Otto's *nude* scene," Allison titters. She's teasing me again.

"Then when it comes time to put it all together, the editor will be able to make the best movie possible," David adds

"But in the end, doesn't the editor still have to do whatever the director says?" Russel asks.

"Sure," David says. "But most editors are pretty smart. And they can be damn persuasive. It's a lot harder to cling to bad ideas when you see a movie put together the right way. Maybe we can even get an ally of ours in the editing room." At that, he looks at Ethan, who nods.

"And who knows?" Allison adds. "Maybe between now and then, Gabriel really will die."

Everyone laughs, and I can't help feeling a little resentful that she managed to pull off basically the same joke that I bombed with. Is it because she's a woman? Or a better actor?

"What about the dailies?" I say, mostly to David and Ethan. "Won't Gabriel see them?"

"Not with a little creative accounting," David says. He looks to Ethan. "We know who we can trust among the crew, right?"

Ethan nods. "And we can tell the different cast members on a need-to-know basis. Am I right in assuming the actors all see Gabriel the same way we do?"

"Everyone I've talked to," Allison says, and Ying nods along with her. "I love this whole plan, by the way. Very power bottom." Allison looks toward me.

"Why do you keep saying that?" Russel says to her, confused.

David ponders it. "I think I get it. The director is the top, right? So if you're the bottom, and you want to take control of the situation, you have to figure out how the director ticks. Right?"

"Right!" Allison says, both impressed by David and exasperated with the world at large for not seeing this obvious truth.

David's comment surprises me because I know he used to be married to a woman. Is he bisexual? Or an open-minded straight guy?

Either way, I'm loving how this whole plan is coming together, and I can't help but feel proud that I'm the one who thought of it.

"Let's trade contact info so we can all keep in touch," I say.

And so we do.

Later, in the car ride home, I say to Russel, "Can you believe it?

"What?" he says.

"That we have *Clayton Beck's* contact information in our phones."

He gives me a smile like a whisper.

"What?" I ask. "Are you worried about the plan?"

"Yes. No. I don't know."

"We don't have to do it if you don't want," I say, not really meaning it.

He nods. "I know. And I wouldn't have agreed if I didn't want to." He doesn't sound like he means it either.

"What about refusing to play by their rules?" I go on. "Remember? We were going to rewrite the rules of Hollywood because we're too nice, and people were walking all over us?"

"Yeah, and if I'm honest, I'm getting a little tired of you bringing that up all the time."

"Sorry." Feeling stung, I look down.

But I sense Russel staring at me. "What we're doing?" he says. "It's exactly the kind of thing I said we should do all those months ago. And back then, I thought I really believed it. But now that we're actually doing it, it feels...weird."

I blow air out through my nose. "I know. Getting Clayton Beck's contact information is the least weird thing that happened tonight. But our plan is going to work."

Russel doesn't look convinced.

"It is," I say. "Just you wait and see."

"Okay," he says, but now his smile is even softer than a whisper, and I'm pretty sure he doesn't mean this either.

That night, I call Greg again, but this time I'm even less forthcoming than before.

I'm not exactly sure what I've gotten myself into.

My first day of filming in Malta comes two days later. It's Dodge's introduction, the sequence in the marketplace that ends up with him seeing his face in that double-sided mirror, where it looks like he no longer has scars. When we rehearsed this back in Los Angeles, Gabriel had said the scene was about the self-hatred of a guy with scars on his face, and the pity the audience was supposed to feel for him. But I'd managed to convince him that, no, it was more about the righteous anger of a character who's been unfairly judged his entire life, and we wanted the audience to feel empathy more than anything.

I had a pretty clear memory that I'd convinced him. He'd said something about how I probably knew more about the character than he did. But that was a long time ago, in a galaxy far, far away, and I had a sneaking suspicion that he might have changed his mind since then.

So the day before, when I received the call sheet listing the shot, I'd texted all my fellow spies from our meeting that night in Valletta. We'd met in a restaurant near the hotel, and I explained the situation, that this might be one of those times where we might have to film a scene twice: the way Gabriel insists on doing it, and then the non-boneheaded way.

The entire sequence is being shot on a soundstage at Malta Movie Studios. When I arrive, I see that the warehouse has been divided into three different sets: the public restroom, which is just an alley where people pee; the market, which is indoors but looks like it's outside; and then the mirror workshop. This sequence will be shot in chronological order, and I'm really glad, because these scenes really do have a very specific build.

I go to the Hair Chair for hair and makeup, then head off to my dressing room to get into my costume. Since the start of the shoot, I've been disappointed that my costumes haven't included underwear from the time period, like you're always hearing about on movie shoots, to help the actors get into character. What would medieval underwear even look like? I've been meaning to ask Russel, but for the time being, I have more important things to worry about. When they call me, I return to the set. They're just finishing the lighting. As usual, they've hired a stand-in for me, and he looks more like me than the guy they hired back in England: same body type, but exact same hair color this time too. As he walks off the set, I nod and give him a high-five, and he nods back, but barely taps my hand, and I wonder if he's jealous that I'm the guy who gets to be in the movie, and he's only the stand-in, even though he doesn't have any scars on his face.

First, we'll do a run-through of the whole sequence, and then we'll rehearse, because everything looks and feels different with a completed set.

But before we do any of this, Gabriel pulls me aside to talk it through, showing me the storyboards again. And when he gets to the part with the double-sided mirror, he says, "Okay, this is the spot where we're going to rip the audience's heart out, remember? The point where we see how much Dodge hates the way he looks, and how he'd do pretty much anything to be the unscarred person in the face of the mirror in front of him."

In other words, he's forgotten our earlier conversation, exactly like I thought. Or maybe he changed his mind.

So I remind him. "I think we talked about this back in Los Angeles. Remember? How the scene isn't really about pity and self-hatred, but that it's more about anger?"

Gabriel scans a clipboard, barely listening.

So I push harder. "I think you even said something about how I had a pretty good take on this character because...well, you know."

He's still not hearing me, but he grants me a glance. "Otto, I did think about what you said. But in the end, I decided we should do it my way. Now let's do a run-through, shall we?"

So much for Phase One of our little operation. Since that didn't work, it's time to move onto Phase Two.

Russel is sitting off to one side, pretending to be on his phone, but I know he's listening in.

He puts his phone away and steps up to Gabriel. "Um, word with you?" By now he knows not to argue with Gabriel in front of the cast and crew.

As Gabriel and Russel talk, I turn away—and find myself facing Aaron, who's also on his phone. He immediately looks up at me, and gives me a curt little nod, and I have a feeling that he was listening to Gabriel and me too. Like Russel, he was only pretending to be on his phone. Aaron's skin looks flawless in the bright lights of the soundstage, almost glowing, and I'm so paranoid that I wonder if he didn't plan for me to see him this way.

A few minutes later, Gabriel returns and calls to the crew. "Okay, let's get started." He looks at me with unblinking eyes. "We're going to do it the way I said."

It sounds like Phase Two—Russel trying to change his mind—didn't work either.

So I have no choice but to smile at Gabriel, and say, "Okay, let's do this."

* * *

The scenes in the alley and marketplace go pretty well, if I do say so myself. We rehearsed with the other actors back in Los Angeles, but they hadn't been in costume, and I hadn't realized how imposing they would be. It also helps that the alley set looks incredibly real, with this trench that looks like it's full of real disgusting stuff. They have extras with these little devices that make it look like they're actually peeing.

Finally, it comes time for the scene with the mirrors. The workshop set looks amazing too. Beautiful and dark, and a little bewildering. It's supposed to be a place where mirrors are made, so there's a work area with tools and raw materials, but it also doubles as a kind of shop with finished mirrors. Some have frames of wood, silver, or gold, and some are hand mirrors or table mirrors. There's even a row of full-length mirrors, like for princesses and baronesses, each one a little different.

Standing on my mark, I gaze around the set, seeing my own reflection surrounding me on all sides, moving in sync with me. It's haunting.

We go through the blocking one more time. It can be really difficult to work with mirrors on film, because they can reflect the lights and cameras—things you don't want the audience to see. So I have to hit my marks exactly. But the moodiness of the set, with all the darkened mirrors reflecting my face back at me, makes it easy to get into the moment.

Then it's time for the actual shot.

"Quiet on the set!" someone shouts.

"Rolling," the DP says.

Different crew members respond, signifying that they're ready to shoot—camera and sound.

Then someone knocks the clapperboard, which helps the editor distinguish the different takes from each other. And Gabriel calls, "Action!"

On that cue, in character, I stumble into the shop, breathing heavily, like I've just picked the lock and ducked inside.

I start toward the back of the shop.

But I realize I'm surrounded by reflections of myself, and I stop.

I turn around in the darkness. On every side of me, in every kind of mirror, my own reflection stares back at me.

I shake it off and hurry on.

But then I stop again. I've seen one particular mirror: the folded one that reflects in on itself, creating a kind of infinity mirror effect.

I step closer, following my marks, which are spelled out with little bits of white tape on the floor. But of course it's not obvious that I'm looking there.

The two halves of my face merge into one image.

A face without scars.

It's a good-looking face, but unnatural, and not just because it's too perfect, with both sides exactly the same. It's unnatural because it's not me.

And I'm suddenly not in character. I'm no longer Dodge the thief—I'm Otto Digmore.

I realize I did this exact same thing as a teenager, holding a mirror up against the non-scarred side of my face to try and see what I would look like if I'd never had my accident, if both sides were normal. How did I not remember doing this when I memorized this scene, and earlier today as we've been rehearsing with the mirror? I guess I saw the image, but I didn't really *look* at it.

It's the image that triggers the memory. Being fourteen years old in the bathroom in front of the medicine cabinet.

I feel now what I felt back then. And yeah, it's some sadness and self-pity.

But mostly it's anger.

I don't show this. I use the emotion I'm feeling, but I channel it into a different emotion—the sadness and self-pity that Gabriel wants me to show. I'm not sure if I'm Otto Digmore, or Dodge the thief, but I'm trying to give my director what he asked for.

"Cut!" Gabriel calls, meaning the scene is over. I stand taller, breaking character.

"Very good, Otto, very good," my director tells me.

I nod. It was good because I'm a professional actor, and I know what I'm doing. I don't think my performance fit the character or the scene, but I did it Gabriel's way anyway. Because I'm an actor, and he's the director, and that's the way it's supposed to work. It's my job to give him what he wants.

And also because I'm waiting for my close-up. That's the shot they'll use for this part of the scene anyway, so it's the one that really matters.

We do a couple more wide shots, and then it is time for my close-up. Before the shot, I look over at Russel and Ethan, standing in the shadows with the rest of the crew. Then I glance at David, leaning in toward the camera. He nods once.

This is Phase Three. We planned all this the night before, right down to the second, in case Phase One and Phase Two didn't work.

"Action!" Gabriel says.

And I do the scene again.

I step forward toward the folding mirror, and the two sides of my face merge into one unscarred face.

I stare at it. The camera is on me, moving in close, but I ignore it, trying to stay in the moment, feeling sadness. And self-hatred, exactly what Gabriel asked for.

"Cut!" Gabriel calls. "Let's print and move on."

At that moment, a lot of things happen at once.

Ethan steps up to Gabriel, pretending to have a note, but really to distract him.

David keeps the cameras trained right on me—and running.

I instantly shift my performance, from sadness and self-pity, to something real.

Now I *am* in character, and in the moment too. On some level, I remember all the times I looked into mirrors at a kid, seeing myself as I might have been. But I channel that emotion into my character—different from me, outside myself, but somehow inside me too.

I feel anger—no, fury this time. Rage at the unfairness of the world, at people's ignorance, and also at my own stupidity and powerlessness. I can't remember the last time I've been so clearly in character, and the moment has felt so right and so real. The emotions gush up in me like water in a fountain, pouring out through the expression on my face.

Gabriel glances my way. Out of the corner of my eye, I see the movement, and I sense the confusion on his face.

The gush of emotions inside me stops, almost instantly.

I'm Otto Digmore again. I look at Gabriel and smile warmly.

His forehead furrows. Did he miss something?

I thought my acting was good before, giving the director exactly what he asked for even though it felt totally wrong to me. But that was nothing compared to what I'd done just then—giving the performance Gabriel wanted, then clicking over into the performance that was right for the scene, then turning that off too, in order to look completely casual when Gabriel looked over at me.

The Academy has given Oscars for less.

My eyes skim over David, Ethan, and Russel, all still clustered by the camera. They're putting in pretty good performances too. They look casual and natural—even Russel. Aw, shucks, here I am on a movie set, nothing unusual going on, and I'm definitely not working on anything behind the director's back.

David nods to me again.

Hells to the yes, he got the shot we needed. Part of me can't believe this boneheaded plan of mine is working. Somehow David and Ethan have managed to get the rest of the crew on our side too, or at least looking the other way. Only Gabriel seems to be completely in the dark.

Back behind the camera, Russel gives a happy little grin and a discreet thumbs-up.

But right then, I notice someone near him, someone who isn't smiling. No, he's looking right at Russel and his thumb.

Aaron.

How much did he see? How much is he noticing now? The rest of the crew is already moving onto the next shot, working to reconfigure the camera and lights.

But Aaron is still looking back and forth between Russel and me, trying to make sense of what he saw.

If we're very smart and disciplined, we might be able to fool Gabriel for the next seven weeks.

It won't be so easy to get it past Aaron Sigler.

And I feel like an idiot that I didn't think of this before.

CHAPTER TWELVE

A few nights later, Russel and I go for a walk along the water. Malta is mostly some big rocks—the different islands—plopped in the middle of the Mediterranean. There's no beach where we're walking, just a short drop directly to the sea, which laps the stone under our feet. Across the bay, dusky towers rise up from behind the ancient limestone walls of the city of Valletta. Everything looks so old, like we really have been transported back to the Middle Ages. Except for the fact that the walls are now lit by the splash of different colored spotlights.

"It's funny," I say, looking down. "Every time I come down here, it seems like the tide is always at the same spot."

"There are no tides in the Mediterranean," Russel says.

"Really?"

"I guess there's a little tiny one. Like, a couple of centimeters. It's because the opening at the Strait of Gibraltar is so narrow. Not enough water goes in and out."

"How do you know stuff like that?"

"Read a lot, I guess."

Then he sighs. I wonder if he's worried about our plan. About Aaron.

"What?" I ask. We don't have any secrets now.

He shakes his head.

"No, really," I say, "what's wrong? Is it our thing with the shoot? Because it seems like it's going pretty well so far." This is true, although Gabriel hasn't tried to do anything truly stupid since the scene in the mirror shop.

"It's not that," he says.

"Then what?"

He stops, and I stop next to him. Together, we stare out at the water, at the yachts and schooners that are heading into the different marinas, seeking haven for the night. Somewhere nearby, the ocean slops, making a loud sucking sound.

"I was reading the news earlier," he says.

"Yeah? What happened?" Russel reads the news way more than I do. I try to stay informed, but I mostly read headlines. And Twitter. But if someone sends me a video, I'll watch it.

"That's just it. Same ol', same ol'." He thinks for a second. "Do you ever feel like the world's coming un-done?"

I'm not exactly sure what he's getting at, so I shake my head.

Russel searches for the right words. "It's just that every time I read the news, it's all so depressing. It feels like everything's going straight to hell."

"You mean Trump?" I ask.

"Sure, he's a huge part of it. But lately, that feels like a symptom, not a cause. I mean, what does it say about a country that it would elect someone like him?"

I scoff. "I know. But there's another election soon."

"Yeah," Russel says, not sounding very hopeful.

"What?"

"I don't know." A briny breeze blows in off the Mediterranean. "For the first time in my life, it feels like evil is winning. Like evil *will* win. Bullying, and cheating, and lying—it all works. Government, the press, religion, even democracy—it's all been corrupted. So how do we solve the world's problems? These days, we can't even agree what our problems *are*. There's no such thing as 'truth' or 'facts' anymore. All we have now are opinions, and it's the people who scream the loudest who get all the attention. Not that any of it matters, since everyone's only talking to their own little bubble anyway. Everyone knows what they know, so everyone's screaming, and no one's listening. And I'm not sure how to live in a world where it feels like there isn't any hope."

Maybe Russel and I still do have some secrets. I wasn't expecting him to unload like this, and I'm not sure what to say. It's not like I completely disagree with him, but he does sound kind of alarmist. As long as I've known him, Russel has had a tendency to over-think things. Hasn't the world always been a crazy place? But somehow we survive. And even if this time it's different, don't we have to figure out a way to carry on? To somehow live our day-to-day lives? Then again, I've also always known that Russel is a very gentle soul. The fact that he's so sensitive is probably the reason why he can't ignore what's going on.

Finally, I say, "I hear what you're saying, and I'm freaked out too. But you can't live your life like that. Sometimes you need to...not ignore it exactly. But put it in the background."

Russel looks at me for a second, and I see that he's as confused by me as I am by him.

But then he picks up a rock and throws it out into the water. And when he turns back to look at me, the gloom is gone from his face. "You're probably right. Hey, what say we get some gelato? I think I saw a place not too far back."

The good news is that Gabriel never mentions the word "slapstick" again. Russel tells me that he and the others are working hard behind the scenes to snuff out the worst of his new ideas before they make it to set.

The bad news is that plenty of his other ideas still get through. We actors usually know what to expect, because we heard most of it during rehearsals back in Los Angeles.

In these cases, we do what we did before. First, we try a little on-set wheedling, and if that doesn't work, we secretly film the correct take behind his back. We quickly realize that the best option is to wait until Gabriel leaves for the day. Then, with a sympathetic skeleton crew, we can refilm almost any scene we want, and take as long as we need to do it. Once or twice, outsiders ask what we're up to, but David is always quick with a reasonable-sounding response.

Even so, we have to pick our battles. The longer the shoot goes on, the more actors we have to bring into the fold, and the more we risk someone accidentally— or deliberately—spilling the beans to Gabriel. It's probably only a matter of time before he finds out, but every time we manage to pull off some new trick, it feels like we're on a winning streak with a slot machine, and we'd be fools to walk away now.

Two weeks later, I look at the call sheet for the following day, and I see that we're filming inside a real castle about a half hour from the hotel, a place called Mdina.

One of the scenes—not one I'm in—takes place on the way from the throne room to the treasure chamber. To hide from some guards, Benjamin and Felicia duck inside a wardrobe together. But it's a small space, and guards are searching nearby. Worse, a maid keeps adding more stuff to the closet, forcing Benjamin and Felicia closer and closer together.

They're both terrified, but there's nothing they can do. At the same time, they're made to confront their attracttion to each other, so it's a nice step in the development of their relationship.

That night, I get a group text from Clayton Beck. By this point, we've all been texting a lot, but I still get a little thrill every time his name pops up.

Anyone up for roast rabbit? he writes. Rabbit is a local delicacy, so this has become our code when one of us wants to get together and plot strategy.

A little while later, we all meet in our usual restaurant, in the quiet courtyard out back.

"He wants me to have a goddamn *gleam* in my eye," Clayton Becks says of the way Gabriel wants him and Allison to play the scene. "Like I'm enjoying copping a secret little feel."

"And of course he wants me to *glare* at him," Allison says, "like I'm a blushing fucking violet, all outraged and offended."

"And then I pretend nothing happened," Clayton Beck adds.

Russel groans. "Oh, good God. Nineteen eighty-six called, and it wants its gender dynamic back."

"Right?" Allison says. "It's like fucking *Pillow Talk*. Of *course* he wants this entire movie told from the point of view of the man."

This time, it takes me a second to realize what they're talking about, but I clue in pretty fast. Gabriel's direction might sound like another small deal, but it completely changes the tone of the scene. For one thing, it's all about that tired stereotype where men are wolves and women are the prey. But even if you flip the genders, it still seems pretty tired. And, frankly, creepy, since one of them is groping the other without their consent. And then when they object, they gaslight the other person about it.

The more I think about it, the worse it seems. Russel is right: it might have played to audiences in the 1980s, maybe even the 90s, but it won't play now. On the contrary, it's exactly the kind of tone-deaf scene that could easily go viral, screwing up the success of the whole movie.

Once again, Gabriel is determined to ruin everything.

We all agree he needs to be stopped, and if he can't be, then we need to get an alternate take. The problem is, we're filming the scene at an actual castle, and it won't be possible to return to this location once they've moved the cameras on to the next scene.

"We tried to talk some sense into him during rehearsal," Clayton says. "But this feels like a hill he's willing to die on."

"And when I mentioned hashtag-MeToo, it made him even more determined," Allison says. "Someone's got a fucking skeleton in *his* closet."

Part of me is surprised that even Clayton Beck is forced to take direction he doesn't agree with. It's no wonder the really big stars, people like Tom Cruise and Sandra Bullock, end up working mostly in projects they produce themselves.

We quickly come up with a plan.

And the next day, I have my driver take Russel and me to Mdina. I don't have any scenes that day, but since Russel is often on the set anyway, it doesn't seem that strange he brought me with him just to observe.

First, we watch as Allison and Clayton film the scene the way Gabriel said he wants it. They also try a strategy that I wish I'd thought of before: doing a lousy job. All morning, they both look awkward and tentative, with a deliberate lack of roguishness on Clayton's part, and Allison doing an imitation of a dead fish. This way, when the editor is confronted with the different takes, they'll be even more likely to steer Gabriel toward the one that isn't completely tone-deaf.

Finally, clearly exasperated, Gabriel says, "Let's take ten!" He said ten minutes, but that usually translates to about fifteen or even twenty.

Right away, he storms off the set. About half the crew wanders off too. The craft tables are down by the restrooms, both a long way away. This is a really good thing.

Allison and Clayton, and the rest of the crew, stay behind. This is the opportunity we've been waiting for all morning. And the instant Gabriel and the others are gone, David and his skeleton crew start filming the scene the right way. But it's a complicated scene, and we only have, at most, twenty minutes. Probably less since people will start returning before that.

Something nags at me, but I can't quite figure out what it is.

Then I realize: when Gabriel called to take ten, Aaron wasn't on set. He's Gabriel's assistant, not an essential crew member, so he comes and goes as he pleases, like Russel. But if he left before he knew about the break, that means he could come back at any time. Especially if he's off in a strange part of the castle, taking a call or something.

As Clayton and the others film their scene, I walk over to Russel, who's guarding the door, waiting to give the signal when he sees Gabriel's return.

I lean in and whisper, "Aaron wasn't here when we broke."

His eyes widen. He knows exactly what this means.

We step out into the hallway—and instantly run into Aaron coming our way.

For a second, we both stand there staring. We were worried about him coming, but neither of us expected he'd show up quite this soon.

"Aaron!" I say, stepping forward, heading him off— stopping him in the hallway. I can't whisper anymore, because then he'll know something is up, so I can only hope that we're far enough away that our voices won't screw up the shots too bad. "Just the person I wanted to see."

He looks amused. "Oh?"

But of course he's the last person I really want to see, and I have nothing to say to him.

I'm worried he'll see the truth in my eyes, so I look at the ground.

"Your shoes!" I say. "You got those here in Malta, right? Where?"

They really are great. It's a pair of Giuseppe Zanotti sneakers, with the trademark zipper and everything.

Aaron can't help puffing up a little. It makes sense I'd notice, since I dress pretty well myself.

"Over in Sliema," he says, "at The Point Shopping Mall. A place called Segue."

I look over at Russel. "Oh, we totally have to go. Can't you see yourself in something like that?"

"I can see *you* in something like that," Russel says, playing along. He nods down at his feet, wiggling his toes in his shoes, and we all look to see that he's wearing a pair of cheap New Balance sneakers.

Russel shrugs haplessly, and Aaron and I laugh together. It's almost like we're having an actual connection, even if it's at Russel's expense.

"Well...." Aaron says, meaning he wants us to step aside.

And we do, because it would be really suspicious if we didn't. At the same time, I'm racking my brain, trying to think of some way to stall Aaron longer.

And then Russel says, with this oh-so-casual tone in his voice. "Hey, you guys, notice how the stairwells are a clockwise spiral?" He points to a nearby stairwell—a spiral one leading down. He looks completely casual too, not nervous at all. "That was by design, as a way to defend the castle."

At this, both Aaron and I look at the stairwell.

"How so?" I say, playing along. Suddenly, Russel and I are doing improv.

"Guess!" Russel says, a little impishly, and I know he's stalling for time, but he still sounds completely real. He even waggles his eyebrows. Turns out he's a better actor than I've given him credit for.

"Because it's easier for people at the top of the stairs to fight the people below?" Aaron says. He's not playing a game—he's actually interested in what Russel has to say.

Russel nods sagely. "Close. And that's true too. But look at the *direction* of the spiral."

Aaron turns to look, but I meet Russel in the eyes so I can give him a little smirk.

"Any ideas?" Russel asks.

"The stairs curve upward from the right," Aaron says, working it out in his mind. "But what difference…? Ah, most of the attackers would be right-handed, which means their sword hands would be up against the interior curve of the wall, and they wouldn't be able to swing their swords."

"Yes!" Russel says, seemingly delighted by the answer. "But *all* of the attackers would be right-handed, because being left-handed was considered evil back then, and so almost everyone was forced to train with their right hands whether it was natural for them or not. And the guards at the top of the stairs would be right-handed too, but they're fighting in the opposite direction, so they have the advantage. Now that I've called your attention to it, you'll see it's an element in almost every castle ever built. Although, interestingly enough, there's a castle in Scotland where all the stairwells are reversed, and it's because it was built by a proud, mostly left-handed family."

Now I'm impressed by Russel's acting ability *and* his knowledge of medieval castles. Then again, he's already proven he's done his research.

Aaron stares at the steps a little longer, then smiles at us and gives a little shrug, then starts forward again.

Behind his back, Russel and I gape at each other like outraged mimes. We're both clearly racking our brains again, trying to think of something else we can say to get Aaron to stop. But the bar is higher now. If we say something stupid or random, it'll make this whole interaction seem suspicious.

And why did we let Aaron pass us by? Now we can't even give the others a couple of seconds warning.

Aaron reaches the open doorway and stops suddenly. "Wait a minute."

He whirls around.

Russel and I step forward together, desperate to do damage control. How much has he seen? How bad is this going to be? Is there any way to keep him from telling Gabriel?

"The doorways all open inward," Aaron say evenly. And I realize he's not looking at us, he's checking out the doorway behind us. Before, he'd been looking at that first doorway too.

"Yes?" Russel says, tentatively.

"So they can always be barred from the inside, right? That's another castle defense." Aaron grins with self-satisfaction.

Russel and I move close enough that we can see through the open doorway, into the set beyond.

They've stopped their secret shoot. It looks exactly like any set would look on a ten minute break. Clayton stands in the middle of his entourage, just like always, and Allison is staring at her phone, looking simultaneously bored and engrossed. David is fiddling with the camera, and Ethan has his back facing us while he's talking on the phone.

I know this is all a total performance, but I'm impressed. Russel isn't the only one who can pull it out when he needs to.

Russel meets Aaron smile for smile. "That's exactly right. Very good eye! When you know what you're looking for, you can see that almost every part of a castle was built with defense in mind."

Aaron doesn't look suspicious in the slightest. Why would he? There's nothing to be suspicious about. And when Gabriel returns, he isn't the least bit suspicious either.

"Clayton? Allison?" he says. "Can I get a word?" Gabriel is still determined to get the shot he wants.

It's funny that Russel and the others all look so calm and collected, because I don't feel that way at all. My heart flutters, and I'm flushed. It's true that we managed to outwit Aaron this time—pretty masterfully, I admit. But it was still a really close call—easily, the closest one so far.

And because of that, it now feels like it's only a matter of time until we get busted.

171

CHAPTER THIRTEEN

But we never are busted. We make it all the way to the end of the shoot, and Gabriel never figures out what we're doing. It's the one upside to his being kind of dim, I guess.

Somehow Aaron doesn't figure it out either.

Before I know it, it's the night of the wrap party. For most of the no-budget indie films I've done up until now, the wrap party has been picking up a keg and ordering pizza at someone's house. But *Blackburn Castle* is a big, splashy studio movie, so we have a big, splashy wrap party. They rent out a whole restaurant, and pay for a huge buffet and an open bar. Most of the actors in smaller roles have already gone home, because even the studio will only pay for so much, but all of the leading actors are here, except for the actor who played Gordo the Magnificent, whose wife took a spill the day before and had to be taken to the hospital for observation.

Actors always say you get really close to people really fast when you're making a movie. Well, it's true. Acting makes you vulnerable, and being vulnerable makes you open to new friendships. Plus, you spend so much time sitting around—in hair and makeup, or waiting for them to set up the next shot—you have no choice but to get to know the other actors, and at least some of the crew. I've lost count of the number of sentences I've spoken to Clayton Beck, and I now even have a couple of good talk show anecdotes.

The other thing actors always say about working on a project together is that while you get really close to people really fast, you drift apart just as fast. That's what happened to the cast of *Hammered*, my old TV series. But I don't think that will happen here, at least with Allison, Ying, David, and Ethan, because we all share a secret.

None of us mentions it directly at the wrap party. As far as we know, we've gotten away with it, so why screw it up at the last second?

But it's the subtext to almost everything we say to each other.

"It was really great working with you," Ethan tells me. "You brought an interesting perspective to the story, and I have a feeling it's going to be, uh, important to the finished project."

Later, Ying leans in, and says with her trademark minty breath, "I loved the choices you made. You really pushed me to do things I never would have done otherwise."

And later still, Allison says to me, "Your nude scene? That's going to fucking *blow* everyone away. And I'm not just talking about your hot little bod."

Okay, not everything is subtext. I try hard not to blush.

"You are *such* a power bottom," she goes on, and a couple of people glance my way. If I kept from blushing before, that's impossible now.

At one point, Gabriel gives a little speech, and his words feel like they're full of subtext too, even if he's not aware of it.

"It was an honor and privilege," he says, choking up right from the start. "I am humbled by what everyone brought to this production, the talent, yes, but also your determination to make this the best possible movie we could make. People say that film is a director's medium, and God knows there are plenty of directors who run their sets like King Gilbert runs his kingdom. But I hope I wasn't like that. I hope I earned your trust like I said at the start. If this movie succeeds, it won't be because of me. It'll be because of the efforts of all us together. Because you let me be the best director I could possibly be."

As soon as Gabriel is finished, I catch sight of David on the other side of the room. I'm dying to have a good laugh with someone about all the double meaning in Gabriel's speech, and I haven't said goodbye to him yet either, so I head his way.

He looks weirdly flushed. My first thought is: Is he having a heart attack? Which is probably weight-ist or something, but it's what I think.

"Are you okay?" I say.

He pulls me aside. "Gabriel is editing the movie himself."

"Can he do that?"

"On the first cut, he can do anything he wants. Apparently, he's got a home editing studio. And a friend to help him."

"What does that mean?"

David runs a hand over his shiny bald head. "It means I had to delete all our extra footage." Before I can object, he glares at me. "I didn't have any choice!

Once Gabriel saw it, he'd know what we did, and he'd tell the studio, and that would be the end of all our careers."

"But that means…"

David nods. "Everything we did was for nothing. And now the movie is back to being one hundred percent Gabriel."

I need to tell Russel. But as I'm looking for him, Clayton spots me from within his entourage.

"Otto!" he says, motioning me over.

Even now, I can't resist drifting his way.

"Hey, Clayton."

"I just wanted to say how much I enjoyed working with you. You have some really great *ideas*."

More subtext.

But then he goes on. "You're also a really terrific actor, and I hope we get to work together again. But even if we don't, let's stay in touch."

"Thanks," I say, a little overwhelmed. "I'd really like that."

I spot Russel at last. But suddenly, I'm in no hurry to tell him what I know. Instead, I ask Clayton what he's working on next, and he tells me all about the upcoming remake of *Logan's Run*.

I can wait a little while longer before crushing Russel's dreams.

For the next month and a half, I feel almost nothing but bummed. I'm back in Los Angeles with Greg, and I'm getting more call-backs than I've ever gotten in my entire career, because everyone knows I have a decent-sized role in an upcoming studio film, and it could turn out to be a big hit.

But I don't get any offers. It's like the whole town is waiting to see how the film turns out, just like Russel and me.

I think back on when I was waiting to find out if I'd be cast in *Blackburn Castle* in the first place, how agitated I was. This doesn't feel like that, because back then at least I had hope. Now it feels like the sun is dying in the sky, and I'm the scientist who knows no one can reverse it.

Speaking of which, I never do tell Greg exactly what went on during the shoot—the part that Russel and I played, I mean. All Greg knows is that Russel and I think Gabriel screwed up the movie. I feel terrible that I'm not being more honest him, and really lonely, but I don't want him paying a price for anyone we did, so I figure the less he knows, the better.

Then out of the blue, David texts us all.

Gabriel sent me a copy of his rough cut.

My heart rises all the way up into the back of my throat. That's never happened before, and it's like I can really feel it.

Before I text back, Russel does. **How bad?**

I haven't watched. I figured we could all watch it together. Roast rabbit anyone?

That night, I join Russel, Ethan, Allison, Ying, and yes, Clayton Beck at David's apartment. The first thing I learn is that DPs must not be paid very much, because his place is a shithole, and smells like burnt popcorn and cat pee. Then again, David's probably on location a lot, and he did recently go through a brutal divorce.

The second thing I learn is that Gabriel's cut of *Blackburn Castle* is bad.

I mean, of course it is. How could it be any different? We were all there on the set, and we watched him make a whole series of stupid choices.

The introduction of Dodge? The first part plays okay, when I'm being chased by guards, but the scene in the mirror studio is all wrong, played totally for pity. It's almost like a *Saturday Night Live* sketch, and I'm embarrassed to be a part of something so trite.

My nude scene? Of course he uses the take from the wrong angle, and it barely shows any skin at all. We see the top half of my torso, and all my scars, but not enough of my body to make much of an impact, so the whole scene is underwhelming, and it does almost nothing to turn a guy like me into a sex symbol.

The scene with Benjamin and Felicia in the wardrobe? Shockingly tone-deaf, and also poorly acted, even if they did it on purpose.

The scene where I overhear the two of them being flirty over the forge in Benjamin's workshop is okay, if only because Russel's dialogue is so clever. When I look over at Mika in the marketplace, it's pretty good too, but that's because I was power-bottoming at the time.

But the rest of the movie is bad. Except it's not terrible-bad. It's only mediocre-bad. I've seen plenty of worse movies. It won't end our careers outright, but it won't make any of us stars either. Unfortunately, since this is probably the one and only chance for someone like me to *be* a star, it's kind of the same thing.

For a long moment after it's over, no one says anything. What is there to say? It's like when you accidentally use salt rather than sugar in a cake recipe, and you cook it all up, and it's not until you taste it that you realize what you've done. You've ruined dessert, and there's nothing you can do except start over. But in the case of *Blackburn Castle*, there is no starting over. There is one forty-five million dollar cake, and it's already baked.

Finally, Allison says, "Maybe the studio will demand a re-edit."

"With what?" I say. "They don't have the good footage."

Silence again.

"Let's think about this for a second," Ying says. "I know he didn't make the movie that any of us wanted." She tips her head toward Russel. "Or that you wrote. But is it 'bad'? I mean, for what it is?"

It's a fair question, so we all give it some serious thought.

"Yeah," Allison says at last. "It's bad."

"Bad," Russel says quickly.

"Bad," Clayton says.

"Bad," I say.

"Bad," David says.

"Bad," Ethan finishes.

Since it's unanimous, Ying bows her head a little, acknowledging defeat.

We all think on it a little longer. It occurs to me that plenty of bad movies go on to be huge hits anyway—guilty pleasures or whatever people call them. But this doesn't seem like that kind of movie. It doesn't feel like a cult movie either. It's not campy-bad, or outrageous-bad, or even maudlin-bad. There's nothing for weird people to love.

We all inhale at almost the same time.

Ying fiddles with her little tin of breath mints, and the pellets rattle inside. "Well, that's that," she says, almost a chirp. "It sucks, but now we know. Now we can all move onto other things."

Which is true: she *can* move on to other things. She's been in lots of other studio movies, and she's probably going to do a lot more. She's in demand. Allison and Clayton too. As for David, if *Blackburn Castle* flops, it will hardly affect his career at all. No one blames the director of photography for anything except if the movie looks bad. It could probably put Ethan in producer jail for a while, but hey, he still got a studio movie made. It's not like it is for Russel and me, where this is the first real break in both our careers, and probably our last breaks too.

"I wish there was some way we could do our own cut," I say. "Just to give the studio another option. Except we already deleted the footage."

David fiddles with an earlobe, then looks over at Ethan. "When will Gabriel be submitting his cut to the studio?"

Ethan shrugs. "Probably not for a few weeks at the earliest. And he'll want your feedback, right? You could string him along. But what difference does it make?"

David doesn't answer for at least ten seconds. Then he says, very quietly, "I only deleted the footage off the studio's server. I backed up the stuff we shot on my own. But just the extra stuff—I don't have the rest of it. And I don't have access to the other stuff anymore."

Once again, I remember Mo's advice to me, all those months ago, about how we all have a choice in how we react to the things that happen to us in life. And those choices determine who we are.

This is also what she meant.

So I say, "We can't give up that easy. If we don't have the rest of the footage, somehow we have to steal it. Then we can re-edit the movie ourselves."

This is like the time in Malta when I suggested murdering Gabriel. But this time, the reaction is different because now they assume I'm making a joke. People laugh.

Except this time, I'm not joking. I can't let this go, not yet, not after everything we've done. I'm already in too deep.

Before long, everyone else realizes that now I'm serious. One by one, they stop laughing, the sound fading away. Then their smiles slip away too.

David shifts in his seat, and the bare skin of his leg makes a quiet squeal against the vinyl of his chair. Ying clears her throat. Allison takes a swig from her beer. No one is looking me in the eye, not even Russel.

So I talk again, mostly to David and Ethan. "Would they even watch it? The studio? If we did our own cut, I mean."

"They might," Ethan said, as quietly as David was before. "I mean, if your version sucks and they realize you stole the footage, they might have you thrown in jail. But they'll probably watch it first."

Allison takes another swig of beer. "Err, don't take this the wrong way, but this is too much for me. I'm sorry, but I'm out."

This surprises me a little, especially after all Allison's talk about nude scenes and power-bottoming. But as outrageous as she can be, I guess she also knows her limits. Which is okay.

"But if you really do something like that, I fucking hope it works out," she goes on. "And, I mean, I won't say anything to anyone. Ever. Not unless you want me to."

David's skin against the vinyl squeals again. "Me too," he says. "I mean, to both things. I'll give you the footage, but then I'm done."

"Yeah, me too," Ying says.

"Um, yeah," Clayton says, nodding in agreement. Naturally, this disappoints me.

"I'm sorry," Ethan says, not looking me in the eye. "But, uh, I have to go with the others."

But Russel's is the take I'm most interested in hearing, even more than Clayton's. So I look to him.

He's not looking me in the eye either.

I don't push Russel for a response, even when we're alone again out in his car. We're side by side, but Russel doesn't start the engine. He stares straight ahead. I have no idea what he's thinking.

"It's a crazy idea," I say. "I mean, how would we even get our edit to the studio? But I keep thinking about what you said back before all this started. About rewriting the rules of Hollywood?" Then I remember how annoyed he was that I kept bringing that up, so I don't say any more.

Russel doesn't speak, and I still have no idea what he's thinking. It could be anything at all. He could tell me we're both holograms and I've spent my whole life living in The Matrix, and I wouldn't be that shocked.

So I keep talking. "You and I both know exactly what this movie should look like. Most of the footage we need to make that cut exists inside David's computer. And it wouldn't be hard to hire an editor to help us on the sly. We would only need a rough cut anyway."

Still nothing from Russel. I'm talking to the world's first freckled mannequin.

"Yes, we might get caught," I acknowledge. "But at least for me, this movie was my one chance to make it in this town. If it comes out the way it is, that's not going to happen. If we try to make it better, we really might make it better, and then both of us are better off. But even if we get caught, well, I can't believe they'd really throw us in jail. Not for long anyway. So the worst that can happen is that we'll be right back where we were before all this started. Or maybe not, because we'll have been involved in one of the craziest Hollywood stories I've ever heard, and maybe someone will want to turn *that* into a movie."

This last part is a joke, kind of, but Russel still doesn't react to any of it. I don't care—I'm not impatient. I want to do this, but I'm not doing it alone. If Russel turns me down, it's dead and buried forever. There's no way I'd risk Russel's career without a firm okay.

But he doesn't turn me down. He looks over at me with an expression I've never seen before, on him or anyone else. As an actor, I'm trying to make sense of it, to understand it. Weirdly at peace? But it's more than that, like he's seen God. Or maybe it's something darker. If I didn't know any better, I'd say he just decided to commit suicide. It scares me a little.

"I'm in," Russel says, very softly. "And think I know exactly how to do this. How we can get the footage we need."

I hesitate for a moment, considering Russel's weird reaction. Then I decide to go with it.

"How?" I ask.

He shakes his head. "I need to check out a couple of things first. But I'll tell you in a day or two, okay?"

"Okay," I say, and now I'm not even sure what I'm feeling myself. Am I excited or scared?

That night, back at the apartment, Greg confronts me as I walk in the door, "*So?* How *was* it?"

So much has happened this evening that it takes me a second to realize he means the movie. But I know I can't tell him about my crazy plan to steal the footage and re-edit the movie ourselves. If we go through with it, and we're caught, we could go to jail. I'm okay with that, but I'm not okay with Greg going to jail too. The only chance he has of surviving a scandal like this is still if I keep him completely in the dark. If need be, I can even make him throw me under the bus.

"It's…not bad," I say. "Better than we expected."

Relief sweeps across Greg's face like a California wildfire. "Oh, man, I'm so glad to hear that! Can I just say? That is *fantastic*." He's so enthusiastic that it makes me wonder if he hadn't already realized something was going on during the shoot. That there was more to my brooding these past few weeks than just my being worried about how the movie turned out.

"I know!" I say, picking up on his enthusiasm. "Thank *God*."

Greg's own smile vanishes like a magician's rabbit.

I've overdone it. Greg knows I'm lying to him, or at least not telling him the whole truth. That whatever went on is *still* going on. I'm usually a good actor, but he caught me unprepared. I didn't have time to rehearse my lines.

Greg keeps staring, and I think, Please, please, please don't ask me to tell you anything more. Because I need to do this stupid, crazy plan, but I won't be able to if it feels like I'm risking your career too.

"Well," he says at last, "I'm glad you're happy. I can't wait to see it."

Then he slowly turns away, and I love him just a little bit more than I did three minutes before.

I admit I pester Russel via text. If we're going ahead with this thing, we have to move fast. But he tells me not to worry, that he's got everything under control.

Then, two days later, he invites me over to his apartment. He says he's finally ready to reveal his plan.

When I get there, I knock on the door, and hear his voice from inside. "Come in!"

I open the door. I see Russel and his husband Kevin, but they're not alone. They're with a small Asian woman, and a shaggy brown-haired guy in shapeless clothes.

"Min! Gunnar!" I say, recognizing both of them.

It's two of Russel's other friends—well, they're also friends of mine. I've known them since we were teen-agers, but they live in different cities, so I haven't seen them very often.

"Hi, Otto," Min says, her cool eyes taking me in.

And Gunnar comes over to give me a tight hug. "Otto!"

"But what are you guys…?" I start to say.

Then I realize: Min and Gunnar must somehow be a part of Russel's plan.

CHAPTER FOURTEEN

A few years back, Gunnar invented an app called Singing Dog, which emits this high-pitched frequency from your phone that makes your dog bark out "I'm a Yankee Doodle Dandy" like it's singing. Well, sort of. The phenomenon went viral, and the app made Gunnar a millionaire. Then a few years after that, they turned it into this animated series on Comedy Central. It was cancelled after only one season, but it made Gunnar even richer. He's a bit of a dork, with terrible taste in clothing: the kind of guy who probably uses his fingers to comb his hair as often as an actual comb. But he has bright eyes and an open smile, and I love him like a brother.

Min is more of a classic nerd. She wears black clothes to match her thick glasses and straight black hair. I can't decide if she's got a sense of style, trying to own the stereotype, or if she's just given in to it. Either way, she's always intimidated me a little, because she seems a little judge-y, but that's probably on me. In a way, it's kind of cool that she's so uncompromising. For a while, she was helping design the space ship for a planned expedition to Mars, but lately she's been involved in this mysterious AI startup.

I'm very happy to see them both, but more than anything, I want to know how they're going to help us steal the footage.

I look directly at Russel. "They're part of the plan, right?"

Russel's hazel eyes gleam in a way I've never seen before.

"Russel explained everything," Min says, taking charge. "And we've both read his script. There's no *way* we're going to let that director screw it up."

Gunnar shakes a fist, and I'm not sure if he's being ironic or not. "No way at *all*."

"How?" I say.

"Well, the four of us have been doing some research," Russel explains. "Unfortunately, there's no way to hack the studio's server and download the files. We've tried everything, and it's impossible. It seemed like we'd have an easier time hacking Gabriel's home computer system, but it turns out that's impossible too."

I look at Min, Gunnar, and Kevin, and they all confirm this with definitive nods.

"At least not from outside," Russel goes on.

"We think we can download the files if we're *inside* his actual editing studio," Min says.

"But…" I say, "wouldn't that mean breaking into his house?"

"And his security system is crazy," Gunnar says, nodding along. "Seriously, he's got one of the best systems money can buy. I might be able to bypass it anyway, but it's risky. And if we were caught, we'd be caught, well, breaking and entering, which is pretty serious in Los Angeles."

"So...that means it's off," I say. "We can't get the footage." Part of me is disappointed, but another part is relieved.

"We didn't say that," Min says, looking over at Russel.

I'm back to being confused.

"We can't *break into* Gabriel's house," Russel says. "But it'd be something entirely different if he *invited* us inside."

"But why would he...?"

Russel holds up his phone. "He's throwing a party this Saturday, in two days. You got an invite, right?"

Russel is right, I did get an invitation to a party at Gabriel's house. I feel stupid I'd forgotten.

"So you and I go to the party—" I start to say.

He interrupts me. "I didn't get an invitation—you'll have to take me as your date. I'm just the screenwriter, remember?"

I laugh out loud. Once again, Hollywood is rubbing it in Russel's face.

"But yeah," Russel goes on, "you and I go to the party together, and somehow we get Min and Gunnar in too. Then we...steal the footage."

I'm having a hard time keeping up with all this. "And once we have it all, we hire an editor?" I ask.

Min dips her head a little. "Well, Gunnar here has become a pretty good editor."

This does seem like the kind of thing Gunnar would be good at.

"So we're going to edit the movie ourselves?" I say. "In a matter of weeks? Because Ethan said—"

Russel interrupts again. "A rough edit, yeah."

"But we still need to get it to—"

"Disney produced *Singing Dog*," Gunnar says. "I know someone who can get it to the right people."

My head is spinning. I knew Russel was up to something, but I had no idea it would be so well-thought-out. He turned my silly idea into something real, and it's kind of blowing my mind. Like I came over and found Mickey Mouse relaxing on the sofa.

Could Russel's plan really work?

Either way, I'm in. Because I'm still in too deep, and I'm determined to see this thing through.

Russel, Min, Gunnar, Kevin, and I spend the next few days together. It feels like we're working on an end-of-semester college project, except we're really planning a theft.

At one point, I find myself making sandwiches in the kitchen with Gunnar. "So where are you living these days?" I ask him. I know he was doing research on Antarctica a few years back, and he's been traveling all over the world since then.

He slices a banana for his turkey sandwich. "Everywhere. I'm location-independent."

Sometimes talking to Gunnar is confusing, because he doesn't think like most people do. In this case, I'm not sure if this is him being weird, or me not understanding. So I ask, "What?"

"I'm a digital nomad. That means I travel around, all over the world, living in different countries for a month or two at a time. When I work, I work remotely, in co-working places."

I've never heard the term digital nomad before, but I know what coworking is, so I have a general idea what he's talking about.

"And you like it?" I say.

"It's awesome. I've been all over Europe, and Eastern Europe. And Central and South America. And Asia. This year, I'm going to New Zealand."

"Isn't it kind of stressful?"

"Being a digital nomad is a lot less stressful than when I owned a place in Seattle. Like, a *lot* less stressful. My life is pretty peaceful. It's a little bit of work getting where I'm going, but once I land somewhere, I settle in pretty fast. The rest of the world isn't like the United States. You don't spend your whole life stuck in a car."

"That's really cool," I say, meaning it. Being in the UK and Malta was stressful, but that's probably because I was shooting a movie while also secretly shooting another version behind the director's back.

"All over the world, everyone goes to the bathroom a little differently," he goes on, explaining about bidets in Europe, squat toilets in the Middle East, and these little hoses in Asian toilets that somehow you use to clean yourself instead of toilet paper.

Gunnar is exactly as weird as I remember, but I still like him.

A few hours later, I realize that Russel is missing, and I find him in the kitchen too, staring into the freezer.

"Hey," I say.

"Huh?" he says. "Oh, hi." He pulls out an ice cube tray, but it hasn't frozen yet, and the water slops on the floor.

"I'll get that," I say, reaching for the Swiffer mop leaning in the corner.

"Thanks," he says as I clean up the spill.

"Is everything okay?"

"What? Yeah, sure. What makes you say that?" He refills the ice cube tray from his Brita, then puts it back into the freezer. This time, he grabs the one that's already frozen.

I stop him with a hand on his wrist. "Russel, we don't have to do this. Not if you don't want to."

He turns away and cracks open the plastic tray. "I *do* want to. You're right about what I said before. How the rules are made to keep people like us out. It's time to rewrite them."

This is what he's saying, but it's clearly not what he's thinking.

"Russel—"

"No!" He slams the tray on the counter, trying to get the last two ice cubes. But they're stuck, and he faces me again. "We're doing this. We *are*."

I'm about to ask why, but I already know the answer: because of me. He wrote that part of *Blackburn Castle* for me, so people could finally see what I could do. And he's not going to stop until people do.

But that's why I can't stop now either—not just because I want people to see what I can do, but because I want people to see what *Russel* can do. He got me this job, and now it's only fair that I pay him back. The movie he wrote is a lot better than the one that Gabriel made, and I need people to know that, whether or not I ever work in Hollywood again.

I look at Russel, and our eyes connect like a suspension bridge across a bottomless gap. The bridge is made of rope, frayed in places, but still solid. I smile first, then he smiles back.

"Then I guess we're in this together," I say.

"Together," he says. But he turns away too fast. He grabs a bottle of Diet Squirt and twists the top. It opens with a quiet sigh.

And for the first time since I put this latest plan in motion, I wonder if I'm doing the right thing.

CHAPTER FIFTEEN

That Saturday, we go to the party at Gabriel's house.

Russel and I head in together, and Kevin waits in a car out on the street, monitoring us on his laptop and communicating over these mini wireless earbuds Gunnar bought. Now we're just like real spies—or at least spies in movies. Min and Gunnar follow behind us, dressed in black pants and white shirts. We figure Gabriel must have hired caterers, bartenders, and parking attendants, so hopefully Min and Gunnar will blend right in, and everyone will assume they were hired by one of the other services.

Unfortunately, Gabriel has also hired security, which we hadn't expected, but should have, because there will probably be celebrities at the party. Anywhere in Los Angeles where there are celebrities, you also have to have security. Otherwise fans and paparazzi will try to sneak in and take pictures.

This makes our plan even riskier than we thought.

The first guard stops us at the bottom of the steps up to the house. It's the only way inside without activating motion-detectors in the yards, according to Gunnar.

I give him my name, and he looks me up on a list on his phone.

At the same time, Min and Gunnar walk by carrying a bucket full of bubbling dry ice.

This was my idea. I'm in the theater, so I've always loved dry ice, and I'm always looking for an excuse to buy some. In this case, I figured why would anyone have dry ice unless they're working the party?

The guard glances over at them, and sees their catering-like clothing and the steaming bucket.

He doesn't stop them.

Then he finds my name in his phone and nods Russel and me through.

So far, so good.

We step into the wash of the front porch lights, and Russel is flushed. He managed to put on a decent performance that one time in Malta, to distract Aaron, but only because he didn't have to think about it beforehand.

"Try to be nervous," I whisper.

"What?" he says.

"It's an old actors' trick. If you try to be nervous, you can't be. It breaks some connection in your brain. If you find yourself starting to lose control, focus on that—try to lose control. Then you'll be back in control. An acting teacher once said to me, if you intellectualize an emotion, you stop feeling it."

Russel frowns, concentrating. Then he looks over at me, lips pursed. "*Now* you tell me this?"

By the time we get inside the house, Min and Gunnar have discreetly ditched the dry ice somewhere back on the porch. They head toward the kitchen, hoping to blend in with the caterers until the next part of our plan.

Russel and I move deeper into the house, trying to get a better look at the lay of the land. The bar and food tables are outside, around the pool, which means that's where most of the guests have congregated. That's definitely good, even better than we hoped for.

But there's also another security guard milling around inside. Worse, he's staying in the hallway that leads to the bedrooms and personal area of the house— and also the private editing room. That's very bad. And what if there's a third security guard we haven't spotted yet? He might even be roaming around in the back of the house.

Now I find myself feeling nervous. I try the same acting technique I suggested to Russel, stopping a nega- tive emotion by over-intellectualizing it, and it works okay at first, but then I realize I kind of have to pee, and I get flustered again.

Speaking into our earbuds, Russel and I quietly explain to the others everything we've learned.

"We need to get down that hallway," Kevin says, out in the car. "Russel and Otto, you need to create some kind of distraction to draw the guard away."

Russel and I look at each other and nod. We start our way to the pool. But as we cross the front room, we overhear one of the conversations around us.

"I had a cast on my arm *and* a leg. I could barely walk for a month. And the fucker's car? Barely a scratch."

"Oh, that's *always* the way. I was in this sixteen-car pile-up on the one-ten, and the guy who caused it didn't even stop. Look at this, you can still see the scar."

This is normal talk for a Los Angeles party. People love going on about their car accidents. Those kinds of scars, the little, almost-invisible ones, are even some weird kind of status symbol.

Russel leans over and mutters to me, "This is like that scene in *Jaws*, when the men compare shark attack scars. Does anyone ever think about how insane it is, living in a city where literally everyone has been in at least one car accident?"

I can't help but snort. If nothing else, it seems like Russel is relaxing a bit.

"What?" Kevin says in our both our ears.

"Nothing," we answer at the same time.

We reach the pool area, and I spot Clayton and his entourage. I nod at him, and he nods back, which is encouraging, since maybe it means we really will hang out together someday. But he doesn't join us, or nod me over to him, and I'm hoping it's because he suspects we're up to something and still doesn't want to get involved.

Russel and I both dish up food from the buffet, which is impressive even by Los Angeles standards. Real plates and cloth napkins, obviously, and all finger food, which makes more sense at things like this: sushi, and cubed fruit on skewers, and grilled meat and cheese on toothpicks. There's even a selection of little chocolate mousse fudgesicles in a tray of what looks like, yes, dry ice. The caterers are working hard, but I see a spring roll floating in the pool, and no one seems to have noticed.

"Give it up! I know *exactly* what you're up to."

It's Gabriel—and I instantly tense. We haven't even been at the party five minutes, and he's already caught Min and Gunnar.

But no. When I turn to look at him, Gabriel is smiling like a party host, not a guy who's just caught some thieves. He's dressed in all light blue, which is good because all white is a total Los Angeles party cliché. It's a nice look on him, especially the slim oxford shirt with the grandad collar.

"What are we up to?" I ask, wary, but trying not to show it.

"You're here for dirt on the movie," Gabriel says, smiling coyly. He stiffens his spine, standing even taller than usual. "Well, I just finished the first edit, and I think you're going to be *very* happy."

"Ah," I say, deliberately vague. I've seen Gabriel's first edit, and I'm not very happy. Because it stinks.

At this, Gabriel turns to Russel, acknowledging him for the first time. "Russel. I'm so glad you could come."

If Gabriel wasn't a bonehead, I might think this was subtext, his way of saying: We both know I didn't send you an invitation, because you're only the screenwriter, and the only reason you're here is because Otto brought you. But it's Gabriel, so I'm thinking maybe he really is being polite.

"Thanks," Russel says. "You have a great house."

Gabriel basks in the compliment while I catch a whiff of his cologne.

"Light Blue," I say. "By Dolce & Gabbana."

Gabriel's eyes twinkle—I've impressed him. "You're the first person who's noticed."

Russel stares at us, stupefied. He has no idea what we're talking about.

So I lean over a little and say, "Gabriel's brand of cologne is called Light Blue. It matches the color of his clothes."

His eyes shoot open. "Oh! Clever."

It might be Gabriel's first clever idea ever. I kind of wish I'd thought of it.

"I really am glad you came," Gabriel says to me. But then he opens the comment to Russel too. "Both of you." He looks back at me. "I know there was some tension on the set. But I want you to know that I always knew you were doing what you thought was best for the character, and your friend's screenplay." He bobs his head toward Russel, and I nod. Gabriel's right, even though this might be the first time he's ever been right about anything involving Russel's script.

"Anyway," Gabriel goes on, "it all worked out in the end. You gave a really terrific performance, and if I do say so myself, I think the two of us ended up making a really good team."

Gabriel's back to talking nonsense again.

"Sometimes I'm jealous of screenwriters," he says, looking between us. "Of the complete freedom they have to control their characters. But then I realize that screenwriters don't get what I get, which is the chance to collaborate with actors—to see a performance come alive before my eyes. And that's just about the greatest thing in the world."

Gabriel sounds like he's actually a good director, like the experience he and I had was a normal one, and everyone on set didn't see him as a fraud. Is he really this clueless? Over the last few months, Gabriel had sort of become the villain in the story of my life, and now I see that he doesn't see himself as a villain, and so my mind is being blown again.

"It really was an interesting experience," I say. "I'm dying to see the finished film. And I can't wait for the world to see it too."

Gabriel smiles like he's touched by my words, like I've complimented him, even though he'd know I hadn't if he'd listened to me for once.

"Anyway...." he says, even as he starts to tear up, and my mind is further blown. I had no idea Gabriel lived in such a crazy dream world. At the same time, it makes me feel a little guilty about what we're up to behind his back at this very moment. I also wonder if there's anything in my life that I'm this delusional about.

"Enjoy the party," he finishes, reaching out to squeeze both Russel and me on the forearm, then tottering off to mingle with the other nearby guests.

Russel and I glance at each other, and I know we're both thinking, There are no words.

At the same time, I see beyond Russel to the view over a canyon in the Hollywood Hills, then down toward Los Angeles at night. The blaze of the city is stunning, and it hums like an angel's halo, but I'm more concerned with the wooded area directly below the house.

I see my chance.

"Paparazzi!" I call out, pointing down into the darkened trees.

There aren't really any paparazzi. I'm creating the distraction we need to draw the security guard out of the main house.

But Gabriel and the other guests all turn to look. Clayton's entourage steps in front of him, like secret service agents trying to take a bullet for the President, and I think, Have they specifically practiced blocking Clayton from cameras? It's pretty cool if they have.

The security guard appears, pushing through the crowd, scowling down into the trees.

I turn away from Gabriel and the commotion.

"I've drawn the guard away," I say into my earbud. "You guys are good to go."

"Roger that," Gunnar says, and I know that he and Min are on the move, toward the back of the house and the editing room.

The guests still scan the trees for paparazzi, but one by one, they're looking over at me too, since I'm the one who called it out.

"I saw the glint of a lens," I explain. I shrug, hapless. "I'm almost certain I did." But now a note of uncertainty has crept into my voice. No one can ever prove I was lying.

"We're at the door," I hear Min say. "But there's a problem. It's locked. And it's a serious lock too."

"Do you think you can pick it?" I say.

"Pick what?" a voice says.

But it's not Gunnar or Min's voice in my earbud. It's Aaron who has appeared out of nowhere, and is now standing right in front of me.

I'm too stunned to respond.

Inside my earbud, Gunnar says, "Maybe I can use a credit card. Oh, wait, no, I have my pocketknife."

Aaron keeps staring. What did he ask me again? I'm confused by the different voices, and I can't remember.

Russel materializes next to me. "My car," he says to Aaron. "I locked my keys inside earlier." He turns to me and says, "No, I think I'm going to have to call Triple A."

It takes me a long second to clue in, to realize that Russel is covering for me, making it seem like I was talking to him when I was talking to Gunnar. It's a pretty darn good performance.

"Or you can call OnStar," I say. "I think they can unlock it remotely."

Aaron stares a moment longer, then nods out into the yard. "There doesn't seem to be any paparazzi."

"Maybe I was wrong," I say. "But I'm pretty sure I saw a camera."

Aaron keeps staring—but not at the woods. At me. He knows something's off, and now he's like a bloodhound trying sniff out the truth. I should have expected this.

"Eternity by Calvin Klein," I say, because I can't think of anything else. "That's your cologne, right? It's pretty cool that Gabriel is wearing Light Blue while wearing light blue, don't you think? I wish I'd thought of that."

Aaron doesn't answer. He also doesn't smile. He's still staring, like a psychologist trying to make sense of some strange new patient.

"Got it!" Gunnar says in my ear, meaning the lock. "We're inside the editing room."

I force myself not to react, but Aaron is still staring, looking between Russel and me. Russel is doing his best not to react either, but now his whole body is as tight as a fist.

"Gabriel says he's finished his cut of the movie," I say to Aaron. "What did you think? Honest answer."

As soon as this is out of my mouth, I regret it. We're in the middle of stealing the footage from Gabriel's home studio, so why say something that might make Aaron suspect that? On the other hand, it keeps his attention on me, away from Russel. And maybe it'll keep Aaron on the defensive—make him less likely to figure out what we're up to.

Aaron smirks. "So Gabriel told you, did he?" He glances off at the view, then says, "You guys both know the quality of Gabriel's work. You should know by now that he never disappoints."

It's a good answer: deliberately vague, like my response to Gabriel earlier. Maybe it's even kind of an insult. Aaron is smart, and he was on the set more than any of us. He knows Gabriel's a hack.

"Oh, come on," I push. "You can do better than that. What did you really think? Are we going to be a critical darling?"

Aaron refuses to take the bait. "Here's what I do know." He leans in closer. "You two were up to something. On set? Not just you two, but the crew too, at least some of them. Care to tell me what it was? It'll go easier for you if Gabriel hears it from me first."

From offense to defense—wow, that was fast. I was just thinking how smart Aaron is, so I shouldn't be surprised that he knew more than he let on. But I am.

"Come on, 'fess up," Aaron goes on. "It's not like I blame you. Everyone's got an angle in this town. I bet yours is a good one."

I smile lightly. Then boldly, brazenly, I say, "Everyone's got an angle, huh? What's yours?" Mostly, I'm trying to go on the offense again, but part of me really is curious: what *is* Aaron's end game? Is he only in this for the money? Or does he want to direct like everyone else?

"Well," Aaron says, smiling right back, "if I tell you, it's not an angle, is it?" He shrugs. "It's okay. I'm pretty sure I already know what you were up to. And if I'm right, it's not over yet."

Russel flinches, a slight intake of breath.

Aaron's eyes shoot his way, and I'm a little annoyed with Russel. But I know he's doing his best.

Aaron obviously suspects something, but I'm pretty sure he's bluffing some too. If he knew we were in the middle of a heist, he would have said something to

Gabriel by now. He wouldn't be out here verbally sparring with me.

A heist? In a flash, I realize that in trying to steal Gabriel's files, we are currently acting out the plot of *Blackburn Castle* almost exactly. I consider all the similarities. We knew we couldn't get past the security system, like how we couldn't get past the castle walls in the movie, so we'd waited for an opportunity to walk in through the front door. We'd worn disguises. We'd created a distraction to get past the guards. Even the things that had gone wrong are the same: guards in unexpected places and having to pick a lock without the right tools.

All these thoughts make my head swim, like the world is bobbing around me—like I'm that spring roll floating in the swimming pool. It suddenly feels so incredibly obvious what we're doing, like there's no possible way Aaron hasn't already figured it out, and now he's just toying with us.

Then from somewhere nearby, I hear the voice of one of the security guards, and it slices so deep into me it's like I'm being gutted like a fish.

"Mr. St. Pierre," the guard says, "I think you need to come with us. It looks like we have a theft inside the house."

CHAPTER SIXTEEN

It's not Gunnar and Min—that's not who the security guard was talking about. No, a guest at the party, an older actress named Paula Lord, left a pair of studded diamond earrings in the pocket of her jacket, which she stored in the library off the entryway, and now they're gone.

I feel bad for Paula, but this is a huge relief to Russel and me.

But we're not out of the woods yet. Russel and I have followed Gabriel into the entryway, and now I can overhear him talking to Paula.

"You need to call the *police*," she's saying, indignantly shaking her mane. "Those earrings cost twenty thousand dollars!"

"Yes, yes, absolutely, you're right," Gabriel says, flustered, but determined to stay in control of the situation. He turns to the closest security guard. "In the meantime, no one leaves." He whispers the rest. "Except A-list, obviously."

This is so typical of Hollywood. People like Clayton never have to follow the rules either.

Right then, I hear Gunnar's voice in my ear, "We got what we need. We're on the way out."

I turn away and whisper back, "No, stay where you are!" I quickly explain what's going on.

"So what do we do?" Min asks, also in my ear. There's a nervous edge in her voice.

It's a really good question. Once the police arrive, they're probably going to search the rest of the house, and if Min and Gunnar are caught, it's going to look very suspicious. On the other hand, if the two of them come out now, they're going to be looked at much more closely than before, and someone might realize they're not part of the catering or valet service. And the security guard isn't letting anyone non-A-list leave the house now anyway.

Russel steps up to me, his eyes bulging like marshmallows. He's looking to me for answers too. Why wouldn't he? I'm the one who insisted we steal the footage from Gabriel. But I still don't know what to do. It won't work to create another distraction. It would look too suspicious, doing the same thing twice. And if Min and Gunnar try to leave through a back entrance, they'll set off the alarm system in the yard. Maybe they'd get away, but they could also be caught by the police, and then we're all totally screwed.

Blackburn Castle. In a flash, I remember how much our plan to steal the footage is like the plot of the movie we just filmed—how we'd walked in through the front door, worn disguises, and all the rest. In the movie, the heist had worked. I'd forgotten that part before. The thieves had gotten away with the gold.

So was there a way out of the house like how the characters got out of the castle? I think back on what the thieves had done: they'd dressed up like a family of mourners at a funeral, with a coffin on a cart, then dragged the gold right by the guards because the coffin also contained a stinky moose head that made them think it really was holding a dead body.

It's hard to keep from rolling my eyes. A stinky moose head? I can't imagine anything less helpful to the situation we're in now.

But then I have an idea.

"Uh, Gabriel," I say, deliberately sheepish, "I think you have a problem."

He whirls on me. "What *now*?" He's just hung up his phone after calling the police.

"I think someone had an accident." I nod toward the guest bathroom off the front hallway.

He frowns. But he steps toward the room, pushes open the door, and peers inside.

Behind Gabriel, I peek into the bathroom too. The toilet is covered with brown, runny streaks. More dark, wet globs spatter the tiled floor. It looks like someone had a very bad case of explosive diarrhea and didn't clean up after themselves.

Gabriel sags like a leaky inflatable. Paparazzi in the bushes? Stolen earrings? Now diarrhea in the bathroom? His party is turning out to be a total disaster.

Except the diarrhea, like the paparazzi, isn't real. It's chocolate from the mousse fudgesicles in the buffet. I snuck it into the bathroom myself just a few minutes before.

Get it? Mousse, which sounds like moose, as in the stinky moose head in the coffin in *Blackburn Castle*?

Right away, Min and Gunnar appear, also according to my plan. They're still dressed in black pants and white shirts, exactly like the other caterers, and they have paper towels, plastic bags, and cleaning supplies.

"We're on it, Sir," Min says to Gabriel.

As Min and Gunnar go to work cleaning up the mess, Gabriel looks on. He's still sagging, but he doesn't look quite so defeated. He's found a solution to one of his problems at least. Meanwhile, Russel stands nearby, helpfully directing guests to a different bathroom.

In moments, the toilet is sparkling clean again, the mess safely sealed away in plastic bags.

Gabriel looks into the bathroom, impressed. It doesn't even smell, which isn't saying much since it never smelled in the first place. But he doesn't know that.

"We'll get this out in the trash," Min says. This is the other part of my plan. Like in *Blackburn Castle*, it's a way to get the thieves out of the building without the guards stopping to search them.

At Min's words, Gabriel nods once. He straightens his back, standing fully upright again at last.

Better still, one of the security guards has seen his interaction with Min and Gunnar.

They start for the front door, and the guard doesn't stop them. Before I know it, they've disappeared out onto the porch and down into the yard.

A minute later, Gunnar speaks in my ear. "We're out. We made it to the car."

Part of me can't believe my plan actually worked.

But this thing isn't done yet. Russel and I have to stay at the party. For one thing, the security guards aren't letting anyone leave who isn't A-list or carrying a plastic bag full of human shit, and the police are about to arrive. I'm not thrilled about this. I didn't have anything to do with the missing earrings, but I'm up to my eyebrows in other mischief.

Still, I'm an actor. I can convince Gabriel and even Aaron that I don't have anything to be nervous about— that I'm completely innocent. Convincing people that I'm something I'm not is literally what I do for a living.

Beside me, Russel pops a peanut M&M from a nearby bowl. But it goes down wrong, and he immediately starts to cough.

"Are you okay?" I say.

He nods, but he doesn't look okay. He looks distraught, and not just from almost choking on a peanut M&M.

I'm an actor, but Russel isn't. Still, he's pulled off some pretty good lies before. Can he do it again? Because whether or not we get caught today depends on whether we can *both* act like innocent men.

Five minutes later, the police finally arrive. The first thing one of them says to Paula is: "Are you sure you're not wearing them?"

"The earrings?" she says, hesitating. Then she pulls back her deliberately messy shag cut and feels her earlobes.

Yes, her earrings were on her ears the whole time. And no one thought to look.

"Oh!" she says. "I feel so stupid." Then she proceeds to apologize to the police, to Gabriel, and to each of the guests. It's pretty clear she likes the attention, even if it makes her seem like a total ditz. It's been a while since she's been A-list.

As Paula is apologizing, Russel clutches me by the arm. "Now let's get the *hell* out of here."

I sense we're being watched. It's Aaron, all the way on the other side of the room. All the questions he had before? They're still on his face. I'm suddenly very glad he didn't see what happened in the guest bathroom. Something tells me he would have immediately seen through the charade.

"No," I say to Russel. "We need to stay a little longer."

He stares at me, and I see the fear in his eyes, but also the acknowledgement that I'm right. He knows the difference between guilt and innocence too. He knows that staying longer means we're less likely to get busted.

Frustrated, he turns away. "I need a drink."

Russel and I stay almost two more hours. And I get to meet Idina Menzel and tell her how much I related to Elphaba in *Wicked*, so it's not entirely bad.

When we both decide it's finally okay to leave, we find Gabriel, holding court by the bar.

"We have to leave," I say.

"So soon?" he says.

"If we don't get outta here soon, you're really not gonna like the smell o' this place," Russel says.

This is a line from *Blackburn Castle*, what Gordo says to the guards at the gate, talking about the coffin with the moose head inside. Part of me can't believe Russel actually says it. He even nails the voice of the actor.

Gabriel snorts.

It really is the right thing to say. Only a completely innocent person would say it.

Russel is turning out to be a better actor than I ever would have imagined.

* * *

"How long do you think it'll take to get an edit done?" I ask Gunnar, back in the car, on our way down into town.

"It depends on the footage," he says. "But I'll work day and night if I have to. I'll stock up on Clif Energy Bars."

"Clif Energy...?"

"Energy bars have more caffeine than coffee. Most people don't know it, but that's where the 'energy' comes from."

It takes Gunnar nine days, and about five hundred energy bars, to edit the movie. When he's done, we all watch it together: me, Russel, Kevin, Min, and Gunnar.

The introduction of my character starts out really good. The scenes in the urinal and the marketplace are fun and funny—not as broad and over-the-top as Gabriel's version. A better fit for the movie Russel wrote.

Then we come to the scene in the mirror shop, me looking around at the mirrors, being taken aback. It's a much more seamless tone shift than in Gabriel's version.

We watch the shot where I look into the folded mirror, seeing my unscarred face for what is probably the first time.

It's a little disappointing. My performance isn't terrible, but the shot we need is off. We didn't get a chance to do a second take.

Still, it's a good scene.

I realize my nude scene is coming up—me bathing in the stream. In this version, I'm totally starkers, and I'm wondering what that's going to look like. I'm also embarrassed to watch it in front of everyone else. I expect them to hoot and holler, and maybe nudge me with their elbows. And I wonder again what it's going to be like when it's released to the world—if this version ever *is* released to the world.

Then it starts. And it is really strange seeing myself on the screen like that, my body. That's my ass and then I turn and—ohhh—my dick and balls. It's all there, everything on display.

I mean, I don't look terrible, but I don't look great either. It's a better than average body, but I'm a little doughy with hardly any abs. I definitely don't look as good as Chris Pine in his bathing scene in *Outlaw King*. Now I'm wishing I'd worked out more. The shot is from the point of view of Mika, and the whole point is that she's surprised by how good I look. But there's only so much you can do with lighting and filters and body makeup.

But as the scene goes on, I wonder if I might be wrong. The whole point is that Dodge doesn't realize that he's attractive, because no one's ever seen him that way before—they've never seen beyond his scars. But now someone does. At first Dodge is embarrassed, but then he spots Mika's expression, and sees himself the way she's seeing him now. That shifts his perspective.

And it's kind of heartbreaking and amazing.

Russel was right when he said the scene wouldn't play if I'd worked out more, if I had an absolutely flawless body, just like it didn't work in Gabriel's version, when I'm shot from the waist up. This scene is perfect exactly the way it is.

Finally it ends, and I realize that no one hooted or hollered, or elbowed me either.

Russel has tears in his eyes. I have tears in my eyes too.

The whole cut is like these two scenes: it's good, sometimes great, but quite a few of the individual shots are kind of disappointing. There are a ton of continuity errors—little things that don't line up from shot to shot—but that's what you'd expect given the way we shot it, which was in furious three-minutes jags behind the director's back. But it is a rough cut, and the potential is obvious. If we can get the studio to buy into our vision, they'll be sure to spring for some re-shoots.

When it's finally over, no one says anything. Did people like it? To be honest, I'm not even sure what I think. I'm too close to it.

Then Min sniffles.

"Min?" Russel says, touching her on the shoulder.

She turns to us with tears in her dark brown eyes too.

"It's really good. You guys made a really good movie."

I'm surprised because Min isn't the crying type. She's not overly emotional.

But she's right.

"Gunnar," I say, "you did a great job."

"Thanks," he says. "But you guys made it easy—you and Russel."

This version works a lot better than the one Gabriel put together. It just does.

So now it goes to Gunnar's contact at the studio. According to Gunnar, they still haven't received Gabriel's cut, and I'm not sure if this is a good thing or a bad one. Either way, if they don't like our version, they might try to track us down and put us all in jail, at least according to Ethan.

Will they like it? There was a time when there wouldn't have been any doubt in my mind. Yeah, Hollywood is sometimes crazy and frustrating, but talent and quality always win out in the end.

Now I'm not so sure. If talent and quality win out in Hollywood, Gabriel wouldn't have been hired in the first place.

Two days later, I get a text from Russel.
No word yet.

A day later, I get another text.
Still no word.

The following week, he texts.
We need to talk. I'm on my way over.

When I try to get him to tell me via text, he doesn't answer. When I actually call him, he doesn't pick up.

He must have been driving something crazy, because he shows up thirty minutes later, even in Los Angeles traffic, and he lives halfway across town.

The first thing he says is, "They loved it."

"But what about—?"

He nods. "Yeah, Gabriel knows. At first he was completely confused, because he still hadn't turned in his edit. But Aaron figured the whole thing out. Everything we did. And that it was us."

"And Gabriel was furious?"

"Sounds like that doesn't begin to describe it. He insisted they watch his cut immediately. So they did."

Russel doesn't say anything else, just stares at me.

"And?" I say. "What happened?"

He smiles like The Grinch That Stole Christmas. And I know everything I need to know.

"So that's it?" I say. "They're going to release our version? Do reshoots?"

"Gabriel's taking it to arbitration."

Right then, Russel gets a text. He reads it.

"It's from my agent," he says. "He says that Gabriel wants to talk to me. Tomorrow at eleven at his office."

"I'm going with you."

Russel shakes his head. "No. I got us into this. And now I'm going to get us out."

CHAPTER SEVENTEEN

The problem is, Russel didn't get us into this. Yeah, he's the one who first suggested rewriting the rules of Hollywood and doing whatever it takes to succeed. But when he said it, he was just talking. Ranting about how Hollywood sucks so hard, like everyone in this town rants all the time. I was the one who turned it into a plan. And every step of the way, every time Russel started to get cold feet, I was the one who insisted that we keep going. So it's not fair if Russel has to suffer the consequences and I don't. It wouldn't even be fair if we *both* have to suffer the consequences.

Somehow I have to make things right.

First things first: I need to be at this meeting between Gabriel and Russel, but they can't know I'm there.

I know Ethan has an office on the studio lot, so I beg him for one small favor: to put my name on the access list for the following day. I tell him that if anyone asks, we were planning to go to lunch. But I doubt that anyone will ever get that far down into the weeds, even if I am caught.

The following day, I'm back on the Disney lot, but this time I'm the opposite of confused. I know exactly where to go, because I planned it all out the night before.

I'm creating yet another character: the up-and-coming actor Otto Digmore who is appearing in a future Disney production called *Blackburn Castle*, and who has come to the studio to have lunch with a friend.

No one looks at me twice, not even to see my scars.

Ethan's office is far from Gabriel's, an entirely different building. But I have a plan for that too.

I buy myself a small coffee and sit outside Gabriel's office building, on a bench off to one side. If anyone asks, which they won't, they'll see Otto Digmore, wearing the appropriate guest badge, enjoying a coffee before lunch.

But I'm really waiting for Russel. I've come early, long before there was any chance he'd go inside the building.

I nod at anyone who makes eye contact. The last thing I want is to appear nervous. I also barely sip my coffee, because I don't want to have to pee once this thing gets underway.

Russel appears in the distance. From his body language, his wary walk, I can tell he's nervous about the meeting. I wonder if he's even tried that technique I taught him at Gabriel's house.

I duck around a nearby corner, making sure he doesn't see me.

A moment later, I peek around the corner.

No Russel. He's gone inside.

I look at my phone: fifteen minutes before the scheduled meeting. Somehow, I manage to wait until right before the meeting, then saunter toward the doors after him.

Halfway there, I realize the flaw in my plan. What if Gabriel makes Russel wait? That's exactly the kind of thing Hollywood players do to show their power. But if Russel is still in the waiting room, he'll see me, and that'll blow my whole plan.

I look back at my phone. It's now two minutes after eleven. If I go too early, Russel might see me. But if I wait too long, I'll miss the meeting.

My whole body breaks out in sweat. I try my own strategy, focusing on an emotion to make it stop, but I quickly realize that sweating isn't really an emotion.

I keep staring at my phone. It's now three minutes after.

Then I see the answer to my dilemma is right in front of my face: my phone. Russel and I can locate each other. I punch up the app, wondering if it's precise enough to show his exact location.

Yes! His blue dot is on the move—Russel on the way to Gabriel's office.

I stumble up to the front door. It's time to play yet another role.

Out of breath, I hurry up to the receptionist. "Russel Middlebrook just came in here, right?" I don't give her time to answer, just keep talking. "I've got his phone!"

"Okay," she says, unsure. "You can leave it here, and I'll give it to him—"

"No, no, you don't understand," I say quickly. "He needs it for the presentation. With Gabriel St. Pierre? It's okay, I know where his office is...."

I take a step toward Gabriel's office, but then I stop, looking at her with practiced Bambi eyes. Now she can even pity me for having scars on half my face—give me her sympathy. I just want her official okay to keep going, because the last thing I need is her calling Security on me.

She eyes my guest badge. What's happening is unusual, but it all makes sense. And the whole lot is a secured area—I couldn't have gotten inside unless someone checked me in.

Her phone rings, and I know I have her. She waves me forward.

"Okay," she says, and I'm off like a flock of birds.

Upstairs, I burst out into the hallway. Too fast! Russel is down the hallway, right in front of me.

I pull back and wait. I'm ninety percent sure Russel didn't see me.

Cautiously, I peek out again.

The hall is empty now. I approach Gabriel's office. The door is closed, but I expect this, given the sensitive nature of what Gabriel and Russel are discussing.

I stop at the door. Listen. The voices are muffled, but clear enough that I can make out words.

There's no one in the hallway now, but there are other offices, and I can tell there are people inside. I hear muffled phone voices and other conversations. It's only a matter of time before someone steps out.

I pull a little box of paperclips out of my pocket and dump them on the floor. Then I crouch down to pick them up again. It's great the floor is carpeted, because they get stuck in the yarn. It smells like glue and dust.

I hear Gabriel's voice through the door.

"It's not the director's job to listen to the screenwriter," Gabriel is saying. "It's the job of the screenwriter to listen to the director."

"Look, it wasn't personal," Russel says.

"It wasn't *personal*? Of *course* it was personal. I know this is a business, but I guess I was stupid to think the two of us were *friends*." Gabriel sounds truly pained, and I can't help feeling a little guilty. Before, I thought of Gabriel as the villain in my story, until I realized at his party that he didn't see things that way. Now I see that from his POV, we're the villains. It's a sobering thought, but it doesn't change the fact that he's still a lousy director, and his cut of the movie sucked.

"Well, I'm really sorry. But…" Russel hesitates. "I was only thinking of the movie. And the fact is, the studio liked what I did."

"The *studio*," he spits. "What do they know about anything?"

Gabriel has a point. I've been complaining about the studios my whole career.

"Are they doing reshoots?" Russel asks Gabriel.

He doesn't answer right away. "Reshoots are completely standard on a film like this."

I feel bad that Gabriel feels so bad, but the fact is they're doing the reshoots based on *Russel's* ideas. One way or another, Russel's is going to be the version of the film that gets released, and that gives me a little burst of pride. It also doesn't surprise me. When it comes to movies, the studios always get their way in the end. Because they can pay whatever price it takes to make people happy.

Right then, a door squeaks open farther down the hall. A man in khaki Dockers steps out and heads my way.

I'm prepared for this, so I'm instantly playing an-other role—that of Harried Office Worker, someone who stupidly dropped a whole box of paper clips. I duck down, trying to hide the scarred side of my face, because it's distinctive enough to call attention to itself. He might know I don't belong here.

I hear swishing, and a guy in a pair of cheap Skechers loafers walks by me in the hallway. Must be an intern.

When I focus again on the voices beyond the door, I hear Gabriel saying, "...just like I can't stop them from cutting it their way. But I *can* stop you from ever getting a decent job in this town again. You and Otto both."

This makes me catch my breath. Is he making an idle threat? Yeah, studios are more powerful than directors, but directors are more powerful than screenwriters and actors—at least actors not named Robert Downey, Jr. And Gabriel has connections at this studio. Those connections weren't enough to save his version of *Blackburn Castle*, but they might be enough to get me and Russel blacklisted all over town. The price Gabriel wants the studio to pay might be throwing us under the bus. That's a very small price for them.

"No!" Russel says. "Otto didn't have anything to do with this. It was *my* idea—*all* of it. And I told you, I'm sorry. I stepped way over the line."

"*Obviously* Otto was involved. The whole cast must have known. The production team too. All of you gossiping behind my back—*ridiculing* me."

"I talked them into it. I swear! Most of the time, he didn't even know what I was up to. If you want to punish someone, punish *me*."

"When it comes to the cast and crew, I just might believe you," Gabriel says. "I know how things go when you're on location, how it's sometimes the director versus everyone else. And maybe I can forgive all that. But the two of you were there the night of my party—and you were *together*. You stole my files. After I invited you into my home. And Otto *was* involved. It's as obvious as those stupid scars on his face."

I'm kind of glad to hear what Gabriel really thinks of me, because it makes what we've done to him feel less bad. I'm also touched to hear Russel stick up for me, but it doesn't surprise me in the least.

"Wait!" Russel says, totally losing his cool. "Let's just stop a minute. I made a mistake, and I'm sorry. But I can make amends. I'll do whatever you want. How much does the studio know? I'll tell them our edit was mostly *your* idea—I'll tell them whatever you want. And if the story ever gets out, I'll take the blame. I'll say I went behind your back, that I blackmailed people into helping me, and that most of my ideas were terrible. We'll give you all the files back, so there won't be any proof that there even *was* a second edit."

"You'll do more than that," Gabriel says without missing a beat. "You'll quit this industry. I don't ever want to hear your name in this town again. And if you do all that, maybe I *will* leave Otto out of it."

So it's not enough for Gabriel to win. He has to punish Russel too. Maybe he really is a villain after all.

Russel doesn't answer, but it's easy to imagine his face going pale on the other side of that door. Gabriel is asking him to give up the one thing he cares about more than anything in the world.

But finally he says, "Okay."

"Then it's a deal," Gabriel says, and now I imagine his little smirk of victory.

I hear movement in the office—Russel standing up from a chair. The meeting is coming to an end. I have to get out of that hallway, fast, before anyone sees me.

I duck into a nearby office, hoping against hope that it's unoccupied.

It's empty.

I think about what I've heard. Russel gave up almost everything he cares about for me even though I'm the one responsible for the mess we're in.

One way or another, I need to fix this once and for all.

Ten minutes later, after I'm sure that Russel is out of the building, I throw open the door to Gabriel's office.

"Great," he says. "Now you too." I hear the disappointment in his voice, his sense of deep betrayal, and I feel a flash of guilt. He was my director, he cast me in a studio movie, and then I turned on him. When Russel and I first decided to rewrite the rules of Hollywood, I never in a million years thought that I might end up feeling bad about it.

On the other hand, for the first time in my life, I feel like I finally have some power in Hollywood. Russel and I really did make a better movie, and now Gabriel is trying to destroy Russel's career because of it. So I don't feel that bad.

His face is hard as he reaches for the phone. "I'm calling Security."

"I wouldn't," I say. "At least before you hear what I have to say."

His hand stays frozen in mid-air. His fingers don't even quiver. His office smells like pineapple and melon—sweet, but slightly off. He has one of those fruit bouquets on his desk, the kind where they make flowers out of cut melon and strawberries, then put them on bamboo skewers like they're stems.

"I heard what Russel said," I go on. "I'm here to make a different deal, but this isn't a negotiation. You can either take my deal or not. Those are the only two choices."

Suddenly, I'm no longer playing a role. I'm back to being myself, Otto Digmore—the *real* me. He's a complicated guy: he feels both guilty *and* powerful. But maybe that's okay.

"First of all, Russel's not leaving town," I say. "You're going to say you changed your mind. Then you're going to let him do his cut of the movie. You're still the director, but you're going to invite him onto the set with you for reshoots and into the editing room for editing, and you're going to listen to whatever he has to say. You're also going to give Russel all the credit he deserves, both with the studio and when the movie is finally released. But I wouldn't feel too bad. Russel's version is good, and you're still the director, so you'll get plenty of credit. Besides, a little humility never hurt anyone's career."

Gabriel laughs out loud. "Why in the world would I ever agree—?"

"Because if you don't, we're going to tell everyone everything that really happened on this production."

Gabriel keeps laughing. "So what? If anything, people will take *my* side."

"Will they? The director who lost control of his movie?"

His smile disappears. "You can't prove anything."

"Of course we can. We can prove everything. Everyone on that set knows what really happened. You think
there won't be people willing to talk to *Variety*? You
think the entire cast and crew has your back? They
didn't before."

"It's still my word against theirs."

"Is it?" I pull out my phone and hold it up as if I've
been recording the whole conversation. If I was
smart—if I'd been a character in one of Russel's
screenplays—I *would* have been recording the whole
conversation. But I'm not that smart. It didn't occur to
me until right before I held up my phone, after it was
too late to do anything about it.

But I'm still a good actor. If I can't convince Gabriel
I'm recording the conversation, I don't deserve to call
myself an actor in the first place.

"We also have your edit," I say, twisting the knife.
"We can leak it to Buzzfeed, and then people can judge
for themselves which one is the better movie. Even if it
doesn't go full-on viral, it'll still be the scandal of the
year in this town."

He stares at me, and I know this is the real test.
Does he really think his cut of the movie is better? If he
does, he might not care if we leak the two versions. He
might think he'll end up smelling like a rose: lone wolf
director staring down a mutiny on the set, clinging to
his vision in the face of a cast and crew that refuse to
do their damn jobs. If this is how he sees things, then I
might really be screwed.

But I have a feeling that, in his heart of hearts,
Gabriel knows the truth.

He considers everything I've said. His hand quivers
ever-so-slightly, and he notices at the same time I do,

and places his palm flat against his desk. The fruit flowers bob a little on their skewers.

One moment bleeds into another, and I think about the risk I'm taking with my career. Gabriel might be petty enough to take Russel and me down even if it ends up hurting him too.

Then I look down at my own hand, and I'm not shaking at all. No matter what Gabriel says, I'd do the same thing all over again. Ten minutes ago, Russel risked everything for me, so the least I can do is risk everything for him back, and nothing could ever feel better or more right. Even if I do destroy my Hollywood acting career, it won't matter, because some things are more important than that. As for the rest of it, whether it was wrong to go behind my director's back, well, I can figure all that out later.

"So you want to blackmail me too," Gabriel says at last. "Just like Aaron."

My first thought is: It's rich being accused of blackmail by someone who was literally just trying to blackmail my best friend.

My second thought is: Aaron is blackmailing Gabriel too? Did he also threaten to release the story of what happened on the set?

Gabriel interrupts my thoughts. "Okay," he says.

I open the door, turn, and in my most commanding voice, I say, "One more thing. Don't tell Russel. This is between you and me." Then I step out over all those paper clips on the floor.

As I'm walking down the hall, I see Aaron in the doorway of his own office, leaning against the jamb.

225

The expression on his face stops me cold. His face is a shifting kaleidoscope of smirks.

Does he know what happened in Gabriel's office? Maybe he listened outside the door, like me. Or maybe he has the office bugged—that wouldn't surprise me.

Either way, he's impressed. I can see it in his eyes. I'm not sure what to think about that, if I should feel proud or what. I do know I like Aaron's John Smedley polo. Unlike that intern before, Aaron's a good dresser.

"What did you get out of it?" I ask. I'm talking about his blackmailing Gabriel, and I know he knows it. But I'm genuinely curious.

He leans in, giving me a better look at his skin, which is flawless even up close. As always, I'm jealous. "A first-look deal with the studio," he says.

I nod. That makes sense. This was his endgame all along, why he was sucking up to Gabriel: he was waiting for the right moment to stab him in the back. It kind of impresses me how cold-blooded he is. It was Russel who first suggested rejecting the rigged rules of Hollywood. And I took him up on it. But we were late to the game. People like Aaron have been making up their own rules for a long time. And most of the time, they're the ones who get ahead.

But running into Aaron is a nice reminder that he and I aren't the same. Even if we both cut corners— even if we were both secretly eavesdropping on Gabriel's office just now—I did it to help Russel. Mostly. Aaron was only doing it to help himself.

Mo was right all those months ago when she said it's the choices we make, not the experiences we have, that make us who we are. In the end, Russel and I got our way, but we didn't end up like Aaron. We're not selfish assholes.

At least I'm pretty sure we're not.

"Call me," Aaron says. "I think you're going to have some heat after *Blackburn Castle*, and I've got a script that would be perfect for you."

"I don't think so, Aaron," I tell him. "But good luck with whatever you do."

I start forward again, and this time, I don't stop until I reach my car.

EPILOGUE

It's almost a year later, the night of the Oscars, and I'm nominated for Best Supporting Actor. Since its founding, the Academy of Motion Picture Arts and Sciences has nominated sixty-two actors for playing disabled characters. Before now, exactly two of those actors have had a disability themselves: Harold Russell in *The Best Years of Our Lives* in 1947, and Marlee Matlin in *Children of a Lesser God* in 1987. If you consider me to be disabled, and I do, I'm the third.

Go, me!

It's been pretty crazy since the movie was released—in August, which turned out to be the right time after all. It was a solid hit, making two hundred and fifty-four million dollars worldwide, which is really good on a forty-five million dollar budget.

It was an even bigger critical hit. Ninety-four percent Fresh on Rotten Tomatoes.

I was a dark horse to be nominated for an Oscar—a very, very dark horse. But people weren't completely shocked. Out of all the actors in the movie, the critics did single me out. And it was mostly because of the two scenes that Gabriel was going to screw up: the one with the mirrors, and—yeah—the nude scene in the stream. That second scene ended up becoming a huge thing, exactly like Russel and Allison predicted it would.

It was definitely strange at first, having the whole world know what I look like naked. Even now, when you Google my name, that's, like, the second photo that comes up, unless you're on Safe Search. When I die, they'll probably use that screenshot in my obituary.

Still, a lot of people got exactly what we were going for, the layers to the scene. How moving it is. The critics loved it, and more than one person has written that it's the best male nude movie scene ever. The only people who don't like it are straight men who are threatened by it. Of the ten negative reviews of *Blackburn Castle* on Rotten Tomatoes, nine of them are written by men, and every single one of them mentions that nude scene in a negative way.

But can I make a confession? Just talking about it on "hot guy" level, not an artistic one, I kind of like the reaction to that scene. I said before I never saw myself as a sexual being because no one else ever saw me as a sexual being either. But now it's impossible not to see myself that way. Me, the guy with scars on half his face! Not just a sexual being, maybe even an actual sex object. Years ago, when I was on *Hammered*, *People Magazine* told us they were considering naming me as one of the One Hundred Most Beautiful People, but then the show was cancelled, and they never did.

Well, this year, I finally made the list. And unlike before, it didn't feel like a "pity" choice, like they were trying to make a point about how the traditional standards of beauty are too narrow. I know for a fact that people find me sexy because people tell me that all the time. Sometimes in public, girls scream when they see me. Women hit on me. Men do too, even though I'm still not openly gay as a celebrity. Greg and I have decided I'm going to come out, especially since there are rumors about me now that people finally see me as sexy, but we're going to wait until after all the Oscar stuff dies down. That's why I'm going to the Oscars with Russel, not Greg. I didn't want to introduce Greg as anything other than my boyfriend. Besides, it turns out Greg was right and a lot of journalists picked up on the media angle about how Russel the screenwriter wrote this great role for his best friend, the actor who had such a hard time getting decent roles in Hollywood.

I go to the gym more than I used to, I'll tell you that. If I go to the beach, there are five paparazzi and thirty random beach-goers waiting to take photos of me in my trunks, to see if I still look as good as I did in that movie.

I've still never worn a Speedo, but who knows? Maybe someday I will. The next time I'm in Europe. People have already seen it all anyway, so what do I have to lose?

Blackburn Castle was also nominated for Best Editing, which is hilarious because it should be Gunnar up for the award. Instead, it's Gabriel and the studio guy who helped him. Yeah, technically they reedited the movie, but the studio made them use Gunnar's cut as their guide, also using Russel's ideas for reshoots.

Gabriel's up for Best Director too. I mean, of course he is, right? It so figures.

Russel isn't even nominated. Unlike Gabriel and me, he's gotten barely any attention at the different awards ceremonies. Not even a Golden Globe nomination. But this also figures. Except for a few embarrassed straight men, everyone likes *Blackburn Castle*. And more than any other person, Russel is responsible for everything good about the movie. And yet three of the five Best Original Screenplay nominations are for pretentious arthouse films that I had a hard time even finishing. This is another Hollywood rule I'm starting to hate: for a screenplay to be good, it has to be really weird or "important" somehow. It's not enough that a screenplay is inventive, perfectly structured, really moving, and wildly entertaining. It's like that stuff barely matters.

But I plan on telling anyone who'll listen—the reporters on the red carpet, and the entire world if I actually win—that Russel is the real reason anyone involved with our movie is here tonight.

I'm not expecting to win. No, really. Every year, there are all these predictions and indicators of who's going to win what award, based on who won the earlier awards of the season. And I've gotten a lot of attention for my performance, and even won two local critics awards, but no one anywhere predicted I would win the Oscar.

It's an honor just be nominated. Seriously, that's enough of a reward.

But then the ceremony begins, and I'm sitting there in the audience, and they come to my category. Charlize Theron is the presenter, and I think, Well, maybe I *will* win. I mean, no one thought I was going to be nominated either. I barely hear any of her cute banter.

Then she reads the names of the nominees, including mine, and I'm so nervous that no mental technique can make it stop. I'm also thinking, Why didn't I pee before my category?

Finally, Charlize Theron opens the envelope, smiles, and calls out, "Timothy Drake!"

I really didn't win. Instead, it's the actor who plays the father in *The Tulip Vase*, which is a movie I was actually up for. I auditioned for the leading role, which went to Miles Teller, who wasn't nominated. I was really bummed I didn't get the part, but now I wonder if that isn't an example of how a rejection can actually be a good thing, because if I'd gotten it, I might not have been able to do *Blackburn Castle*. *The Tulip Vase* is a good movie, but not as good as *Blackburn Castle*. *Tulip* is one of those movies that a lot of people like now, but it won't be remembered in five years. *Blackburn* feels like it could maybe become a classic.

And hey, did I mention it turned me into a sex symbol?

Later, in a major upset, Gabriel wins Best Director, beating out Julian Lockwood for *The Tulip Vase*.

I'm the only other high-profile nominee from *Blackburn Castle*, so they have a camera on me when Gabriel wins. I smile big and clap heartily. It's not a terrible performance, but nothing like the one I gave in *Blackburn Castle*. Or, more importantly, the one I gave the night of Gabriel's party, or that day in his office. And unlike the people around me, I make a point not to give him a standing ovation. Read into that what you will, TV viewers.

Next to me, Russel is clapping too, but the cameraman completely ignores him, because he's only the screenwriter.

In my mind, I try to make sense of what's happened. A mediocre director created a so-so movie and was too boneheaded to know it, so Russel and I had to film extra scenes behind his back, then break into his computer and steal his files, so we could re-edit them into something good. And then we had to blackmail him to make him use our cut.

That man just won the Oscar for Best Director.

Then again, there's no other way this story could have ended, is there? I'm not a writer, and even I can see that. When men like Gabriel fail, the system somehow makes it so they succeed anyway.

At the start of this whole movie journey, Russel told me that Hollywood was completely unfair, and I'd agreed with him. But I hadn't known the half of it.

Up on stage, Gabriel thanks a long list of people, including Clayton and Allison, but not Aaron, and also not Russel or me, or Ethan or David, since he figured out they were in on it too. This is clearly deliberate, and he's pushing the terms of the deal he agreed to with me. But I'm not going to say anything because I kind of admire him for finally figuring out how to throw some decent shade.

After the ceremony, out in the lobby of the Dolby Theater, Russel and I run into Julian Lockwood, the British director of *The Tulip Vase*. We both stayed at his house in New Orleans when I auditioned for his movie—a whole other story.

His face lights up.

"I want you to know, I voted to nominate both of you," he says, reminding us he's a voting member of the Academy. He looks at Russel and says, "You were robbed. *Blackburn Castle* is one of the best scripts I've ever read."

Russel blushes.

Then Julian Lockwood looks at me and says, "*You* should have won. I voted for you, and I got all my friends to vote for you too."

"Thanks," I say. "You should have won too."

Russel nods heartily.

Julian Lockwood tilts his head, and a smile lingers on his lips. He knows there's a story here, because we're very pointedly speaking out against the director of our own movie, which isn't done unless there's a very good reason.

Russel and I both offer back smiles so mysterious they would put the Mona Lisa to shame.

"Anyway," he says. "You're both big Hollywood players now, and I wanted to make sure to remind you that I told you so." He says this directly to me.

I laugh out loud. "You did *not!* You told me that the odds of someone like me making it as a movie star were ten million to one."

"Ah, but I also told you to stick close to this one, didn't I?" He jabs his thumb at Russel, and now the smile on Julian Lockwood's lips is the one that's putting the Mona Lisa to shame.

And I realize he's not wrong: he saw Russel right away for the talented guy he is. And much more importantly, the incredibly loyal friend.

"Okay, you're right, you did tell me that," I admit, and Russel blushes again, but also sparkles a little like the glitter in the wallpaper all around us.

We linger in the lobby after the ceremony. For one thing, I'm wearing a sixteen-thousand-dollar Brioni Italian tuxedo, and I want to show it off. For another thing, it's kind of fun to be congratulated by people like Matt Damon and Seth Rogen. Charlize Theron sees me and gives me a hug that is somehow both congratulatory and consoling at the same time. I spot Gabriel lingering on the other side of the lobby, but he must be aware of us too, because our paths never cross. I haven't seen Aaron anywhere tonight. His production company has at least four movies in development over at Disney, including one with Clayton Beck, who hasn't answered any of my texts since I was nominated for an Oscar and he wasn't. But at least Aaron didn't get an invite to the Oscars. It's petty, but that makes me happy.

Finally, it starts to feel like Russel and I are digging for compliments, so I text my driver to come pick us up. Then I say to Russel, "Hold on." I want to use the bathroom one more time before hitting the horrible Los Angeles traffic.

I'm standing at the urinal when I sense a familiar presence next to me.

Gabriel. He's wearing a boring Ralph Lauren tuxedo, but he's also the one holding the damn Oscar. This is like the first time we met, at the urinals on the Disney lot. It's almost too perfect, like something out of a movie.

This time, I'm not flustered at all.

"Gabriel," I say.

He hesitates, surprised to see me. It's like he's scared, which is kind of trippy.

Then, like he's doing something brave, he steps up to the urinal and unzips. I'm really hoping the Oscar slips and falls, but it doesn't.

I finish, shake well, and zip up, but I don't leave. Not yet. Instead, I turn to him and glare, right in his face. I'm tempted to say, "Congratulations on your Oscar," since we both know he doesn't deserve it. But I figure it's more damning to say nothing at all.

Even better, he can't seem to start peeing. Normally, I would never torment a guy who's pee-shy, which can be pretty embarrassing, but this is different. I love watching his cheeks flush.

Finally, I half-snort, shake my head in disgust, then walk on, leaving him behind. I can't wait to tell Russel what happened in this bathroom.

But as I'm leaving, someone else is entering.

I do a doubletake.

It's Steven frickin' Spielberg. He ignores me, but I'm pretty sure it's because he doesn't see me.

But he sees Gabriel.

"Gabriel!" he says, lighting up. "Congratulations, I loved *Blackburn Castle*. Any chance I can get you to come in for a meeting?"

Unfortunately, I make the mistake of stopping in the doorway to watch all this as it unfolds. Right where Gabriel can see me.

And as he's standing there, being chatted up by Steven frickin' Speilberg, he loses whatever blush his cheeks had. I know he knows I'm here, but he doesn't even look at me, and whatever smug satisfaction I'd been feeling thirty seconds before is now stuck in my throat like a chicken bone.

I decide I'm not going to say anything to Russel about what happened in here.

I'm not much of a partier, and neither is Russel, but that night we go to as many Oscar parties as we can manage, including the one thrown by Beyoncé and Jay-Z. I mean, come on. I'm an Oscar nominee, and Russel is the writer of a hit movie. We both even kind of directed and edited the movie too, and we secretly deserve Oscar nominations for those things too. We now both know for a fact that if we're given a chance to show what we can do, we can do solid work. Even under the most bizarre of circumstances.

So the night is a little bitter, but it's mostly sweet. I get to meet almost every celebrity you can think of, including Jennifer Lawrence, Tom Hanks, and Viola Davis. And they want to meet me.

Every time, I make a point to introduce them to Russel and give him all the credit.

But after a while, I realize that lots of people want to talk to Russel even without me chatting him up. Not the other actors so much as producers and directors. Unlike Gabriel, they're not stupid. They know that the most important people in Hollywood *are* the writers, because they create the scripts that make good movies.

At one point, I turn and see Russel talking to Christopher Nolan, who directed *Inception*, *Dunkirk,* and the *Batman* movies. "Have your agent set up a meeting, okay?" he's saying. "I want to hear all your ideas."

But weirdly, while Russel is happy to be with me, he doesn't seem all that excited about setting up a meeting with Christopher Nolan—or any of these offers. Which, if it's a strategy, is a good one, because it seems to make everyone want him more.

Oh, I also get openly hit on by a lot of people—four women and three men. This kind of thing is still really flattering, but I tell everyone, "Sorry—taken."

Which I am. It makes me sad that I can't share this night with Greg, and I realize I made a big mistake by leaving him home. I should have said to hell with it and brought him openly as my date. I'm the person being honored, right? I text to tell him that, and he tells me he was thinking the same thing, but it doesn't matter because this won't be the only time I'll be nominated for an Oscar—that I'll have another chance to show him off. It's exactly the right thing to say.

After a few more hours of being feted and sucked up to, Russel and I look at each other at the same time. And we nod. It's finally time to go home.

We meet my driver, who is so fit and handsome that I'm pretty sure he's an actor himself. I tell him to take us to Russel's apartment first.

"Did you have fun?" I ask Russel along the way.

"My whole life, I've dreamed of going to the Oscars," he says. But then I realize he hasn't really answered the question. Is he jealous that I was nominated for an Oscar and he wasn't? Because if he is, I totally get it.

It's almost five a.m. when we finally arrive at Russel's place.

"Well..." he says, turning for the door of the limo.

But I stop him with my hand on his shoulder. "Russel? There's no way to thank you for everything you've done."

He looks at me with mock-disgust. "Otto! You don't have to *thank* me. I didn't do anything more for you than you did for me."

"But you did," I say, and suddenly I'm on the verge of tears. "Everything that happened, it's all because of you."

Now I am crying outright, and I'm worried that the driver is going to see and maybe Tweet about it, which is something I really don't need right now.

Russel scoots closer to me on the seat, and even though he's not a hugger, he takes my face in his hands and lifts my head up, so we're staring into each other's eyes. "Otto? We're a team. You know that, right? We've got each other's backs, and we always will. If you ever need anything, you know you can count on me. And I know I can always count on you. Always and forever, no matter *what*. Anything at all. Right?"

I love the feel of Russel's hands on my face, one hand on my scars. He even wipes a tear away with one finger.

"Hells to the yes," I whisper.

Russel and I are a team, and I'm not kidding in the slightest when I say that's better than winning an Oscar or working on a project with Steven frickin' Spielberg. Like, way better. Over the years, only around three thousand people have ever won Oscars, but I truly wonder if that many people have had the kind of friendship I have with Russel.

"So why are you crying?" he asks me.

It takes me a second to put what I'm feeling into words. "Because for some reason, it feels like you're leaving."

He pulls his hands back from my face.

"You are?" I say. "You *are* leaving?"

Now he won't look me in the eye. "Not right away. Even I'm not stupid enough to pass up a meeting with Christopher Nolan. But soon…yeah. Kevin and I are leaving Hollywood."

I can hardly believe my ears. But at the same time, it's exactly what I expect him to say.

"But…why?"

He searches for the right words on the back of his fists.

He opens his mouth to speak, but I interrupt him. "You can't leave. You said you were tired of playing by their rules, and so you changed them. And it worked."

"Otto, you did that. And Gabriel will make—"

"No," I say. "You don't need to worry about him."

Russel's eyes pierce me like a lance. "What did you do?"

I don't look away. "You said it yourself: we have each other's backs. This time, I had yours. I swear to you, he won't ever bother us again."

Russel's smile is as warm as the sun. But it doesn't last long. He sighs and looks out the tinted window.

"I don't have any regrets about what we did," he says. "I'd do the same thing all over again in a minute. And I couldn't be happier for you."

"Then…?"

"What we did…made me feel strange. I still agree that the game is rigged, that the rules are mostly just excuses to maintain the status quo. Not just in Hollywood, but everywhere. But lately it feels like *everyone* has decided to stop playing by the rules."

"Isn't that a good thing?"

"Maybe. I don't know. All I know is that it freaks me out."

I'm not sure what Russel means, so I keep listening.

Russel takes a breath. "You know how I've talked about how it feels like the whole world is coming undone?"

"Sure." He's talked about this a lot lately, not just on that seaside walk in Malta.

"I find that terrifying. I've always been an optimistic guy. But for the first time in my life, I feel like the future of the whole world is in doubt. Like we probably won't survive. And this isn't a movie, so there won't be some unexpected third-act twist, a hero to save the day."

"I don't…"

"Doing what we did? Breaking the rules like that? I know I said that's what I wanted, but it was all talk. It's too stressful for me. It makes me feel…bad. Like *I'm* out of control, like I'm not sure how far *I'll* go. Once you start cutting corners, it can be really hard to stop. And then suddenly you're no better than the thing you're fighting against. Do you know when you mentioned murdering Gabriel in Malta, I thought you were serious at first?"

"Everyone did."

"Yeah, but for a split second, part of me wondered if it wasn't a good idea."

"Oh." Finally, I'm starting to understand where Russel is coming from. He really is a decent guy, the gentlest of human souls. He's not made for crossing lines and pushing limits. And honestly, neither am I.

"I'd do it all over again," Russel says with a firm nod. "But I'm not sure I want to *keep* doing it."

"But you've wanted to make movies your whole life."

"And I plan on doing that. Or at least I plan to keep writing them. But I don't need to live here to do that— at least I hope I don't. Kevin and I have talked about this a lot, and we both want our lives to be about something more than the hustle of this place. Because Hollywood *is* a hustle. A constant one. Always cutting corners and making compromises. Maybe that's life for everyone everywhere, but it seems different here somehow. And it's exhausting. You know what I was talking to Christopher Nolan about?"

"This," I say.

Russel nods. "And he says it never ends. He says in a lot of ways, it gets worse. He says if he was just a screenwriter, he'd leave town too. He thinks he'd write better scripts. That this isn't the real world."

Leave it to Russel Middlebrook to be talking existential despair with Christopher Nolan at an Oscars party.

"But—" I start to say.

"Or maybe I can't handle success," he goes on. "I *know* my stomach can't handle it. You've had a stomach of steel through this whole thing. But I'm not brave like that."

I laugh out loud, even as I realize I'm crying again. "You're choosing to leave Hollywood at the height of your success because it's not making you happy? I think that's literally the bravest thing I've ever heard."

He smiles, grateful.

I remember again Mo's advice to me, all those months ago. She told me, "They say that people are the sum total of our experiences, and it's true. But what they don't say is that it's not the experiences that define us. It's the choices we make after they happen."

And I finally *really* understand what she meant. It wasn't that stuff I thought before. It was more about when I was dealing with Gabriel, how I had to decide what to do, exactly how far I wanted to go, every step of the way. And when it was all over, I had to decide if I'd gone too far. I'm still pretty sure I didn't, because I'd done what I'd done for all the right reasons. I went just far enough to keep from being an asshole, even if Gabriel would probably disagree.

Now Russel is giving me another decision to make. And in this case, I'm pretty sure not being an asshole means letting Russel do what he needs to do. Even if I'm really going to miss him.

"What will you do?" I ask. "Where will you go?"

"Did Gunnar tell you what he's doing now?"

"He said he's something called a ...digital nomad?"

Russel nods. "Kevin and I are going to do the same thing—travel the world for a while. See everything there is to see. One of the things I most hate about Los Angeles is that everyone here thinks it's the center of the fucking universe."

"But it's not," I agree. I think for a second. "Can I visit you?"

"You damn well *better*. And I don't mean for, like, two weeks in August. I'm planning on you traveling with us for months at a time. Like, between movies, okay?"

"You bet!" This is the easiest promise I've ever made.

He straightens in his seat. "Well, I should probably..."

Once again, I stop him with my hand. "Russel..."

He looks at me.

"I love you." There. I've finally said it. But it doesn't mean what it might have three years earlier. Now I love him as my best friend, not as an unrequited crush. In a way, the words mean more now.

"I love you too," he says, like it's the most obvious thing in the world. Like it's the truth.

Now there are no more words. I've finally said everything I have to say.

So I hug the world's best best friend, even though he's not a hugger, so long and hard that I can feel the moisture of his body even through the Armani tuxedo I made him wear. I'm pretty sure he can feel my sweat too.

Then Russel gets out of the car and walks away.

And I don't give a flying fuck what the limo driver thinks.

Coming soon!

Russel Middlebook: The Nomad Years

A new series about Russel (and Otto!)
as they explore the world

BOOKS BY BRENT HARTINGER

<u>The Otto Digmore Series</u>
(Adult Books)
* *The Otto Digmore Difference* (Book 1)
* *The Otto Digmore Decision* (Book 2)

<u>Russel Middlebrook: The Futon Years</u>
(Adult Books)
* *The Thing I Didn't Know I Didn't Know* (Book 1)
* *Barefoot in the City of Broken Dreams* (Book 2)
* *The Road to Amazing* (Book 3)

<u>The Russel Middlebrook Series</u>
(Young Adult Books)
* *Geography Club* (Book 1)
* *The Order of the Poison Oak* (Book 2)
* *Double Feature: Attack of the Soul-Sucking Brain Zombies/
Bride of the Soul-Sucking Brain Zombies* (Book 3)
* *The Elephant of Surprise* (Book 4)

<u>Other Books</u>
* *Project Pay Day*
* *Three Truths and a Lie*
* *Grand & Humble*

ACKNOWLEDGMENTS

It breaks my heart a little that this is the last book of The Otto Digmore Series, because Otto might be my favorite character ever, and I've loved writing every word of his story. Who knows? Maybe I'll go back inside his head one day.

In the meantime, it's important to thank the people who helped me bring him to life, especially my husband of sixty zillion years, Michael Jensen. And my agent Uwe Stender, who handles the sordid business of coin.

I'm truly honored that I have such a diverse set of first readers: Erik Hanberg, Brian Katcher, Robin Reardon, and Molly Ringle. They all came at the book from a different perspective, and there was a point where I felt like I was being picked apart by Alfred Hitchcock's birds in *The Birds*. But as a result, it's hopefully a much better book.

Only slightly less important were my generous beta-readers, some of whom have read almost every book I've ever written. Words fail me. Thanks so much, Anthony Braxton, Matt Carrillo, Will Haydon, Julia Huni, Deborah Jacobs, Stevie Jonak, Nick Kotowski, Brad Lane, Doug Lubbers-Moore, Matt Lubbers-Moore, Matthew Morrison, Robert Rice, Tim Sandusky, Gregory Taylor, William Toth, Christopher Udal, and Brandon Will.

Finally, thanks to Philip Malaczewski for the great book jackets, and Anthony Casella and Michael Crouch for helping create terrific audio editions of these books.

Made in the USA
Coppell, TX
21 March 2020